BETWEEN WORLDS 8

A FATHER'S JOURNEY

LORI WOLF-HEFFNER

Dedicated to all factory workers of Waterloo Region, who not only welcomed my family when we arrived in the 1950s but who also shaped our region for years to come.

CHAPTER ONE

If her turning fifteen included Dad's suddenly watchful eye every morning while she ate breakfast, Juliana had very little hope that she would be allowed to get her learner's permit next year.

Juliana loved having Dad home on a regular basis now that he had quit his trucking job, but she could feel his eyes on her as she ate her cereal.

"You have to stop staring at me, Dad. I'm not a baby!"

"I'm just worried about you. You used to eat slower in the mornings. And healthier. Well, usually. Sometimes you eat healthy and slow at breakfast, and sometimes you don't. I'm trying to figure it out. All this variance is very inefficient."

Inefficient. Dad's new favourite word since starting his new job two weeks ago.

Juliana took a deep breath. "There's nothing to figure out. Rachel and I talked for a long time last night, so I'm running late."

Rachel was Juliana's best friend in Calgary. Since Juliana's move halfway across the country to her grandfather's house in Kitchener, Ontario, six months before, they only saw each other online, and the two-hour time difference sometimes made it a challenge. But yesterday had been Juliana's birthday, so they had made the time to chat. Only three hours later, at close to midnight, had Juliana fallen asleep. With final school exams around the corner everyone was too busy to celebrate right now, though her dance friends had thrown her a little party at the studio.

Apparently, Dad still wasn't finished observing. "See? If you'd gone to bed earlier, you would've slept better, gotten up earlier, and eaten slower. It's so simple. I don't get why I didn't notice this before!"

Dad's new job required him to take two college courses: Health & Safety and Finding Efficiencies in Logistics.

"It's at least whole-grain cereal." She carried her bowl and spoon to the dishwasher. "Besides, family nutritionist," she said with a twinkle in her eye, "I eat a wide variety of foods for breakfast. You should be lucky I didn't wolf down cake from the studio birthday party."

"Good morning, sweetheart," Dad said as Mom came into the kitchen.

Juliana rolled her eyes as she always did when her

parents used lovey-dovey language. "By the way, Mom, one of my pointe shoes celebrated my birthday last night too hard and broke."

"You'll need new ones fast—your Father's Day recital is coming up." Mom pulled a bowl out of the cupboard, grabbed a spoon from the drawer, and served herself cereal and milk in less time than Juliana needed to do a shuffle-off-to-Buffalo step in tap class. Juliana did her best to hold back a laugh at Dad's wide-open eyes.

"I don't understand it," Dad said.

Mom's cheeks were stuffed like a squirrel's. "Understand what?"

Dad waved a hand in exasperation. "I thought you were so health conscious all these years, and here you and Juliana are wolfing down your breakfast. I don't get it."

"I'm also practical."

Juliana took advantage of the distraction and rushed out of the kitchen to grab her backpack. But because her grandfather's house was small and the walls and doors were paper-thin, Juliana could hear her parents' entire conversation.

"Who made you foreman of the breakfast shift?" Mom asked sarcastically.

"Kids need their parents to supervise their meals."

Juliana could imagine her mother rolling her eyes. "That's not how it was when you were growing up, and that's not how it was for us either. Our parents were often on different shifts at the factory, so we always fed ourselves, and we turned out just fine without someone supervising our breakfasts."

Juliana heard Opa coming upstairs from his bedroom in the basement. He had let Mom and Dad sleep in his bedroom when the family moved in.

"You're still watching everyone eat breakfast, Paul?" Opa said.

Juliana burst out laughing in her bedroom.

"I heard that!" Dad shouted down the hallway.

"Are you the foreman of this breakfast shift?" Opa asked.

Now Mom laughed. "That's exactly what I said!"

Opa and Oma had worked for many years in a rubber factory in Kitchener. Juliana had never asked Opa about his work, and he had never raised the subject. They talked about his family and his life back in Romania before he immigrated, but rarely about his work here in town.

Juliana zipped her bag shut and rushed out of her room in time to see Mom patting Dad's stomach.

"Why don't you lead by example, Paul?"

Juliana giggled as Dad pulled up his jeans at the waist. "I'll have you know I stopped bedtime snacking after my first Health & Safety class and I've already dropped a pound."

Juliana said goodbye as she ran through the tiny kitchen and down the two stairs to a landing that led to the basement in one direction and out the side of the house in the other.

"Wow, young lady," Dad said. "Those shorts are really short."

Juliana stopped, turned, and looked pleadingly at Mom.

"Paul, she has to get going." Mom waved Juliana out the door.

As the screen door slammed shut behind her, Juliana rolled her eyes. Her most desperate wish had finally come true: Dad now worked a regular nine-to-five job, which meant he was home every day. She had wished for this change for years, especially after dance and school had filled so much of her schedule that she couldn't ride with him on day trips in his truck. But now he was scrutinizing her every move as though she were five instead of fifteen. It'd only been two weeks, and he was already driving her up the wall.

NORMALLY, Juliana loved buying new dance shoes. Pointe shoes were at the top of her list because she had a whole meticulously developed ritual to break them in properly. But where Mom would search online for ways to save Juliana's pointe shoes for just a few more weeks (in case things had changed in the twenty years since she had danced *en pointe* herself), Dad had dived into learning about all the dangers of pointe shoe buying.

With Dad's "safety meter" at a new level of alertness, Juliana had begged Mom to postpone pointe shoe shopping until she was free, but Mom had insisted Juliana go with Dad.

"Besides," she'd said, "it'll help your father see everything you do. He made this change for you, Juliana. We have to let him get used to things."

Dad followed Juliana inside for what she was sure would be the most horrible pointe shoe shopping trip ever. But as she neared the pointe shoe area, her face lit up. She was saved!

"Jasmine!" Jasmine was her best friend from Kitchener Dance Academy. Thanks to Jasmine, Juliana's dancing had improved by leaps and bounds—pun fully intended—in the last six months, and Jasmine had said that she'd even be happy to work with Juliana as a duet partner next year despite Juliana's lack of skill.

Jasmine was blunt that way.

"I broke my shank," Juliana said. A shank was the hard part along the sole of the shoe that helped keep the shoe stiff so the dancer could stay on her toes. "What are you here for?"

"I start at my first ballet intensive the week after school finishes. Mom wants everything ready to go."

"Typical nurse, eh? Always prepared?"

"Yep."

Juliana's dad and Jasmine's mom chatted with each other as the sales associate brought out boxes with pointe shoes for Jasmine to try on. When the sales associate opened the lid, Juliana was surprised. Jasmine's mom was from Guatemala and her father from Serbia, so she always wore caramel-coloured tights and matte-brown pointe shoes. But in the box were ballet pink pointe shoes.

"Switching to pink?"

Jasmine slipped her feet into the first pair, the pink pale against her brown skin, and walked over to the barre where she supported herself as she carefully rose to the tips of her toes under the watchful eye of the sales associate.

"How does that feel in the toe?" the sales associate asked, interrupting their conversation.

"Comfortable."

"Not too loose?"

Jasmine shook her head, and the sales associate pinched the heel of the shoe, measuring to see if it allowed for too much slack. She asked Jasmine to lower into a demi-plié to see if her toes would squeeze in the shoe's box—the hard part that supported the toes while the dancer was *en pointe*.

"And how's the double shank?"

Jasmine rose back onto her toes. Juliana knew it was hard to evaluate the comfort of a new brand of pointe shoe in the store: without the elastic and ribbons on them to pull the shoes tight to the foot, it was a best guess based on previous experience.

"I think I'll be good," Jasmine answered. "I'm doing two ballet intensives and a dance camp this summer. Miss Ambrosia said I'd benefit from the extra support."

The woman nodded and offered another brand for Jasmine to try. As Jasmine switched out her shoes, she answered Juliana's question.

"I use pancake makeup to change the colour."

That explained why Jasmine's shoes didn't have the sheen to them that Juliana's had. Juliana had noticed, but had never asked. She'd just assumed the shoes came that way.

"Can't you get shoes in brown? Seems like an extra step to colour them."

Jasmine walked to the barre and rose to the tips of her toes again. The sales associate pinched the heel of the new shoes. "It *is* really annoying, but if I don't do it I'm limited in the kinds of pointe shoes I can get. Very few companies produce brown-satin shoes."

While Jasmine decided which shoes to buy, the sales associate asked Juliana what she wanted, and Juliana explained her preferred brand and size.

"My arches aren't the strongest," she told Jasmine. "Even single shanks are hard for me to break in. I was surprised when mine broke. My shoes usually last the year, even through the summer."

Jasmine picked up the winning pair and closed the box lid. "I guess it was just a way for your shoes to wish you happy birthday?"

"That's what I thought!"

When the sales associate returned with Juliana's pair, Dad stopped the sales process in its tracks and picked up a shoe to inspect it.

"The tips on those ones are skinnier than on Jasmine's," Dad said.

"I like a tapered box," Juliana said. "It makes my legs look longer."

Not releasing Juliana's shoe, Dad walked over to the wall of pointe shoes and began matching the platform— the tip the dancer stood on—of the shoe in his hand with each one on the wall display. Juliana's face turned hot as Jasmine's gaze travelled to her.

"Before you say, isn't this what I wanted, it is!" Juliana whispered. "I just didn't want Helicopter Dad to replace Faraway Dad!"

Despite Juliana's frustration, Jasmine burst out laughing. "Oh my god, Juliana, that is so sweet!"

Without warning, Dad turned around to Jasmine's mom. "You said you were a nurse? Which shoes decrease the likelihood of Juliana breaking her ankle?"

Jasmine covered her mouth with her hand to stifle a giggle, while Juliana rolled her eyes.

CHAPTER TWO

"You have to sit still if you don't want me to poke your eyes out!" Maria said to Elisabeth.

Elisabeth tucked her hands under her legs as she adjusted herself on her bed in the front room. Maria sat opposite her on a wooden chair she had turned around from the table. "Maybe I should sit on a chair, too, so I don't bounce." The straw in the mattress cracked as she shifted again.

"But it's the perfect height," Maria said. "In the hair salon in Temeswar, the hairdresser was as high as I was when she cut my bangs."

Elisabeth released her hands and parted the hair that hung over her face to past her waist so she could see her best friend. "I don't know if I can do it." She studied Maria's modern haircut. "But I love it on you!"

Maria grinned from ear to ear. "Then let me do it already!" She held the scissors up while Elisabeth pushed her hair over her face again.

Several months before, on a family trip to the beautiful city of Temeswar, Maria's mother had allowed her to cut the hair at the front of her head, leaving her with "bangs" as the hairdresser said they called it in America. The look was fashionable with the rich families—like Maria's—and also in the big, modern cities, like Temeswar, where Maria had even seen telephones and electricity, two things that didn't exist in their tiny village of Semlak. Maria still wore the rest of her hair in a braid attached to the top of her head, like all unmarried German girls in Semlak.

Maria lowered her hands. "But are you certain? Because once I've cut these, you'll be old and grey before they grow back!"

Elisabeth's heart thumped and her skin tingled. "Oh, I don't know! What will Stefan think?"

Maria laid the scissors on the large wooden table behind her. "You're asking this now?"

Elisabeth crossed her arms. "You did ask if I was certain!"

Maria sighed. "I'm nervous about being the one responsible for cutting your bangs! If you don't like it, can we still be friends?"

Elisabeth squeezed her best friend's hands. "Of course!

But now that you've asked again, I do worry if Stefan will like it. That's important."

"Well, has he complained about my hair?"

Elisabeth tried to think of any objection mentioned during any of the many conversations she and Stefan had had over the months, and finally shook her head.

Maria continued. "Konrad has always liked mine even though he's so traditional. He says he likes how my bangs make my face look."

"But Mammi said they're useless and will poke my eyes out when they grow too long."

The girls giggled at Elisabeth's mother's comments. She sometimes worried about the strangest things, though Elisabeth suspected it was mostly that she didn't want things to change.

"But she said you're allowed to do it nonetheless?"

Elisabeth nodded, and then her eyes opened wide again. "But what will Tata think?"

Maria considered the question. "He did write you a postcard and sent it to me in that magazine from America, right?" The magazine had been filled of pictures and drawings of modern American women.

"That's true...and now that he's lived in America since Advent of last year, he's probably used to girls with bangs."

Maria held up the large metal scissors. "So...?"

Elisabeth agreed, sat on her hands again, and told Maria to start.

Maria brushed Elisabeth's thick, blonde hair so that it hung over her face like a smooth curtain, with only Elisabeth's nose poking through.

"This is how the hairdresser in Temeswar did it." Maria placed her hand at Elisabeth's eyebrow and trapped a few inches of hair between two fingers.

Elisabeth held her breath and squeezed her eyes shut once she saw the scissors coming close to her face. A few moments later, Elisabeth heard the snip and opened her eyes.

Maria held a lock of long hair in front of Elisabeth, and Elisabeth grasped it in her hands. Butterflies in her stomach wouldn't stop fluttering. Had she made the right choice? She loved her hair, and holding it this way, separated from her head, made her hold her breath for a moment.

Then she let it out. What she thought about her decision no longer mattered: she couldn't well run around the village with only a chunk of hair missing!

She had placed the lock of hair next to her on her bed and had closed her eyes, readying herself for the rest, when Mammi burst into the room from the kitchen.

"What is it?" Elisabeth asked.

Mammi either stormed into rooms or entered quietly. Angry and serious were her two emotions. But this reaction was one Elisabeth had never seen: Mammi had tears in her eyes. Even when Mammi had had great difficulties with her pregnancy over the winter she had not turned to her daughter for help.

This was very important.

Maria looked away out of respect. "Maybe I should go."

Elisabeth grabbed Maria's hand as though to say, "You can't leave me like this!" She returned her attention to Mammi and pushed the rest of her long hair out of her eyes. "What is it?"

Mammi held a small piece of paper. It looked like a telegram.

But didn't telegrams only come when someone died? Elisabeth's father worked in a cigar factory in America. What if there had been an accident?

Mammi couldn't speak. Elisabeth's stomach rose to her throat. Mammi never searched for words.

She handed the telegram to Elisabeth, who forced herself to read it.

A moment later she jumped up and screamed, startling Maria, and gave Mammi a tight embrace. Then she placed the telegram on the table and resumed her position: back straight as a board, hands nailed under her legs. "Quick! Finish cutting my bangs!"

"Can't I know?" Maria asked.

"If I tell you, that will make two of us who can't sit still, and you're the one with the scissors! But it is good news!"

Mammi wiped her nose using a handkerchief and a moment later her usual demeanour returned. She pointed at Elisabeth's bangs. "Such a useless thing to do with your hair." She left the two girls to return to her workshop to keep making shoes.

As the large scissors neared her eyes again, Elisabeth focused on the crucifix that hung above the doorway. She prayed with all her might that Jesus would give her the strength to sit still.

As Maria cut her hair, Elisabeth's cousin Georg came to mind: this news would make him very happy. Only a few years younger than Mammi, Georg had fought in the great war that had almost torn Europe apart. He now suffered from nightmares. But in her father's absence, Georg had almost become like a father himself. Perhaps sharing this news would offer him some relief.

A MOMENT after Maria announced she was finished, Elisabeth grabbed the telegram, bolted from her chair, and darted out the house door without even inspecting her new appearance in a mirror.

"What's the good news?" Maria called after her. "And where are you going?"

In her excitement to share the news with Georg, Elisabeth had forgotten Maria.

"Lissika!" Maria called as she chased her friend. "Your hair isn't up!"

Something else Elisabeth had forgotten in her excitement.

By the time Elisabeth reached the second gate, Maria had caught up with her and grabbed her by the wrist. "What did it say?"

Elisabeth began jumping up and down but then stopped when two older women walked past her house, their curious eyes focused on the girls. She whispered the good news to Maria, who promptly grabbed both of Elisabeth's hands and jumped up and down with her. The older women scowled at them.

"I have to tell Georg!" Elisabeth said and bolted again. "He needs something happy!"

"But your hair! What if Stefan sees you?"

"I don't care!"

As they ran down the gravel street, lifting their ankle-length skirts just enough to let them run, heads turned. Yes, it was improper for any girl or woman to leave the house with her hair down. Elisabeth imagined her new haircut also met with disapproval. But she was going to explode if she didn't share the news right away.

Georg's wife, Eva, who was only a few years older than Elisabeth, had become a good friend to her. She was expecting their first baby and was scared because Mammi had lost her last one only a few months before. She had to tell Georg and Eva *now*, not only because Elisabeth herself was excited but because she was certain the news would make Georg and Eva happy, too.

Elisabeth turned a corner, running past a row of houses almost identical to hers. Most German homes in Semlak, in fact, looked similar to one another: a three-room house (front room, kitchen, back room) with a cellar at the back followed by a summer kitchen, stalls for horses and cows, a summer shelter for animals, and finally the outhouse. On the other side of the property were the gardens; the *hambar* for storing corn; stalls for the pigs; a shed for the wagon; coops for ducks, geese, and chickens; and the manure pile. Farmland lay outside the village, on parcels of land with their own dwellings called *salasches*.

As Elisabeth turned another corner, Maria's footsteps disappeared behind her. A few steps in and she could see her destination: the other Schuhmacher house. But whereas Elisabeth's property had a shoemaking workshop tucked into the summer kitchen, this Schuhmacher home had a blacksmithing workshop, with a forge inside and a chimney at the top, separate from the house.

"Georg! Eva!" she called as she opened the first gate to her uncle and aunt's property. As was customary, Georg, the oldest son of four grown children, and his wife lived with Georg's parents. Samuel, the younger son, lived with his wife outside the village on the family *salasch*. Georg's sisters, Susi and Gretche, lived in the village with their husbands.

Usually, Elisabeth preferred to not draw her aunt and uncle's attention—they were mean people—but today the happiness inside her silenced her dislike for them.

"Georg! Eva!" she cried again.

Georg came running out of the workshop. A large, powerful man, he wore a heavy leather apron, and his face was stained with soot. That a man his size could move so quickly never ceased to surprise Elisabeth.

"What is wrong?" Georg asked.

Before Elisabeth could answer him, she wrapped her arms around him, startling him.

Eva shuffled out the door at the side of the house, careful of the baby she was carrying inside her. "Elisabeth? What is it?"

Elisabeth gasped for air and her throat burned. Why did God make it hard to speak after running, especially when one had good news to share? She might look that up in the Bible later.

The telegram slid out of Elisabeth's fingers while she still had her arms wrapped around her cousin. "Can I read it?" Eva's voice was gentle.

Elisabeth released Georg from her embrace and nodded, still catching her breath.

Eva's eyes opened wide as she passed the telegram to Georg. Elisabeth hugged her friend, mindful of her bulging belly, while Georg read the telegram.

"That is indeed good news." A gentle smile on his face,

he opened his arms for Elisabeth again and she gave him another hug. Georg rarely spoke or smiled, so Elisabeth took no insult in his quiet reaction, though others often did.

Maria, out of breath and feet dragging, arrived just as Konrad-Bátschi stormed out of the workshop, also wearing a heavy leather apron over a linen shirt and pants.

"Where's my turtle of a son? Get your lazy hands back in here and get to work."

Georg swallowed and turned away from Elisabeth. Her blood boiled knowing the shouting and insults Konrad-Bátschi paid his son every day. Elisabeth had heard it many times and she had also seen her uncle hit his son when his fits and nightmares overcame him.

"Well?" Konrad-Bátschi said. "Or do I need to set off a bomb under those pants of yours?"

Elisabeth and Maria exchanged looks: Georg had once mistaken a children's ball flying through the air for a bomb and had pulled Elisabeth and Stefan to the muddy ground to protect them. Was his father trying to *cause* a nightmare?

Before Georg could answer, Margarethe-Néni, his mother, came out of the house. "What's all this noise about?" she asked. "Georg! Why aren't you helping your father?" Upon seeing Elisabeth, she clapped her hands together in amazement. "Good heavens! Elisabeth Schuh-macher! How could your mother let you leave the house like this? And what have you done to your hair?"

Elisabeth didn't care. She would not let her aunt and

uncle steal her joy today. She blurted out the good news: "Tata's coming home in two months!"

Maria and Elisabeth jumped up and down. Eva's face broke into a grin and she grabbed Elisabeth's hand to share in the joy but kept her feet planted on the ground. Georg's smile grew just a little more, which in his world meant a lot of joy, too.

"That is good news," Konrad-Bátschi grumbled. "Then my family can stop looking after your land."

With Tata gone, only Elisabeth, Mammi, and Elisabeth's three siblings could look after their farmland outside the village. There, they grew grain and corn to feed their family and livestock for the year, as well as some corn for popping, and broom corn to make their brooms. The Schuhmachers also had a small parcel of land near the Marosch River on which they grew grapevines for wine. On their property around their home in the village, they tended vegetables, fruit trees, and nut trees. For animals, they owned several cows, six pigs, and two horses, though Georg's brother and sister-in-law now cared for most of Elisabeth's family's animals on the *salasch*. Although they were landowners and therefore not poor, Elisabeth's family did not have extra money to hire day labourers like Maria's family did, and her siblings were simply too young—Anna was ten, Luki eight, and Rosina six, and Luki and Anna still went to school—to care for all of this with her. Had Georg and his brother Samuel not offered to help care for their crops and livestock, Elisabeth didn't know how her family would have managed everything while Tata was in America.

"Are you going to have a celebration to welcome him home?" Eva asked.

"Oh...I suppose so. I only found out right before I came here, so I haven't had time to think about it."

Breaking out into a huge grin, Maria grabbed Elisabeth by the arms. "I could help you plan it!" Maria said. She looked at Margarethe-Néni's disapproving glare. "But first, we should get your hair up."

The two girls giggled, Georg let another small smile slide onto his face, and Eva squeezed Elisabeth's hand in happiness.

Tata would be home in August, a whole three months earlier than planned. Elisabeth didn't know if she'd be able to sleep a single night until then.

CHAPTER THREE

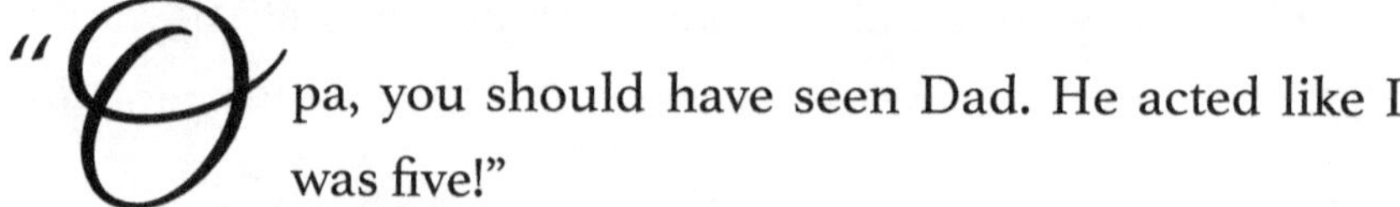

"Opa, you should have seen Dad. He acted like I was five!"

Juliana sat next to her grandfather on the couch in the living room. She had arrived home an hour before, had texted Rachel to tell her about the pointe shoe shopping and replied when Jasmine texted, "Did your dad buy five-foot or ten-foot long ribbons?" Ribbons simply needed to be long enough to cross over your foot and wrap around your ankle twice, but Dad had assumed longer was better, and Jasmine continued to tease Juliana about this.

Opa laughed at Juliana's complaint. "Back when I was in the factory, sometimes a new foreman was like that. Your father is just nervous."

Juliana asked what a foreman was, given that she'd heard that reference a few times this week already, and Opa said it was a man who made sure the line in the factory kept moving.

"A manager?"

Opa shook his head. "Managers worked in the office. A foreman was still part of the union."

Juliana didn't quite get the difference, but it still sounded like a manager to her, so that's what she remembered. Besides, she wanted to complain more about Dad right now. "But this is nuts! It was embarrassing!"

Her phone dinged, and it was Jasmine.

Tapered box or wide box? 😂😂😂

Juliana held up the conversation for Opa to see. "Look! Jasmine won't let it go."

Opa laughed and shook his head. "Yulika, Yulika. She is just teasing. In the factory, we always made fun of each other."

After almost fifty years in Canada, Opa still pronounced the *j* in her name—both his nickname for her and her full name—with a *y* sound even though he would say "just" and not "yust." But Juliana had grown to love it. No one else in the world called her Yulika. Just her grandfather.

"Years ago, this young man joined the factory and he had long, curly hair. Almost right away we called him Cauliflower."

Juliana's eyes popped out of her head. "That's mean!"

Opa smiled his gentle smile. "No, not at all. In fact, he

loved it. I think Karl still speaks with him and uses that name." He rubbed her shoulder. "Your father has always been away. Now he's home with family. This is new. Be nice to him. He's almost like an immigrant."

Juliana laughed. Dad was as Canadian as they came, but he was acting as though this house was a strange, new country.

After the joke wore off, Juliana sighed. "I've only got so much niceness in me, Opa. He hates it when Mom nags him, and now he's doing it to me. He's the adult."

"When Mammi was your age, she was treated like an adult."

Mammi was what Opa called his mother, Elisabeth. She had passed away a long time ago, but Juliana loved hearing stories about her.

"In the church? Because she was confirmed. But she wasn't a full adult until she was married, right?" As soon as the words passed her lips, Juliana realized how odd they sounded: a girl did not become a woman in Semlak until after she was married. She and Opa had discussed that before, but it was not a concept she would ever grow used to.

Opa smiled. "Yes, but everyone expected her to act like an adult all the time anyway. She had to look after her family."

Juliana stared at the floor. If Elisabeth could take care of her family and act like an adult at Juliana's age, why was

Juliana so upset by her father's new behaviour? Was it really that bad?

Opa patted her on the knee. "You can't change Paul. Give him time. You know what? We haven't talked about Mammi's drawings for a while. Why don't you bring me the book?"

Juliana's reaction was her answer: she jumped up and charged to her bedroom to find the leather-bound book her great-grandmother had filled with pencil sketches almost one hundred years ago. Although it had taken Juliana sometime to admit she was happy in her new home, one reason she had changed her mind about the move was learning about her great-grandmother. Over time, Juliana had stopped talking to *Omama* when she held the book privately in her room and instead talked to her as Elisabeth. When she was with Opa, though, she said "Omama" out of respect. But Elisabeth was the closest thing she had to a grandmother since she couldn't remember Opa's wife, Oma, who had died eleven years before, and Dad's parents had passed away before she was even born.

Juliana retrieved the book from her nightstand drawer and returned to Opa as fast as she had left him.

"*Wie der Blitz.*" Opa smiled.

Juliana didn't speak German, but Opa said that sentence often. It meant "like lightning."

"I like talking about Omama."

Juliana opened the book and flipped through the pages she and Opa had already talked about. The book had perhaps eighty pages, but Juliana and Opa had talked about the first thirty drawings or so by now, spending extra time together since Easter.

Opa didn't know the reason for each drawing, and although Juliana wished she could learn each one's actual story, she also found that some drawings simply spoke to her. When Rachel's mother had died in a drunk driving accident several months before and Juliana had felt so angry she was ready to explode, she had been drawn to the sketch of an old lantern. Especially after Jasmine said that she thought the lantern revealed anger, Juliana felt a sense of connection to Elisabeth. It was not something she could ever explain to anyone, and Juliana didn't believe in ghosts and spirits and such, but somehow she felt like Elisabeth had drawn that image just for her.

"What drawing are we at today?" Opa asked.

Juliana stopped at the first one she didn't recognize: a lot of the strokes were dark, as though Elisabeth was trying to express anger again, this time in the galloping hooves of a horse.

"That's strange." Opa pointed to a man's shoe resting in the horse's stirrup. "When Mammi was young, men didn't ride on the back of a horse. They drove from the wagon."

"They used horses and wagons to get around? Like the Mennonites?"

Opa nodded. "Yes. The Mennonites live like how Mammi lived before the war. Even after the war, some lived the old ways. But Mammi always looked to the future."

"The war? World War One?"

Opa laughed in amusement, the way adults do when a kid gets something foolishly wrong. Juliana hated when people laughed at her like that. "World War Two, Yulika. Things changed a little after the First World War when Mammi was your age, but the big changes were after World War Two."

"Did you drive a horse and wagon when you were a kid?"

Opa laughed, and again, Juliana felt like a kid and not the adult she was apparently supposed to be. "Romania was poor, but there were cars. But when Mammi moved back to Semlak with me, we didn't need a car. Semlak was not even five kilometres long. You could walk everywhere. We weren't farmers anymore, either. It was nice for farmers to have a car because their fields were outside the village." Opa appeared lost in thought, and Juliana worried he might begin hallucinating again. It had happened a few times before and once frightened Sophie, Juliana's twelve-year-old cousin. But Juliana hadn't witnessed a hallucination in months now. Maybe his dementia medication was helping?

Opa stood up and rummaged around in the photo drawer in the wall unit. Juliana made a mental note to fish through there sometime herself. She still couldn't find a photo of her great-grandmother, and she longed to see one to make Elisabeth more real to her.

"Yes, this is what I was looking for."

He showed Juliana a warmly coloured photo of a young girl sitting on the hood of a car and a woman Juliana guessed to be Oma holding a baby upright beside the girl. Because of Opa's Alzheimer's, sometimes he changed the subject of conversation without warning.

"Aunt Anne and Mom?"

"And our first car. When Oma and I arrived in Canada, we didn't have money for a car. We bought this house because it was close to the factory and we could walk to work every day. We didn't have to pay for a bus. But the factory paid me so well that I bought a car only a few years later."

Juliana smiled. "So, no horse and wagon."

Opa nodded. "And the cars are much better here than in Communist countries."

Juliana had put off learning what Communist meant, because she didn't care at all for politics. But Opa had used the word so often she finally had searched it online. It meant a kind of government where the country looked after and owned everything. So everyone had a job and healthcare was free, but no one owned a house or a business. But she also learned that these governments functioned under a dictator and that no one in the Communist countries in Europe, like Romania, where Opa was from, could travel outside the Communist zone except in special circumstances. The government controlled everything. They even had secret police. It didn't sound like a nice way to live, and Opa had commented a few times about that, too.

The side door to the house slammed shut, pulling Juliana out of her thoughts.

"Oh my god, Juliana, I am so sorry!" Dad called out to her from the entrance. "Are you ready?"

Juliana rolled her eyes. To her father, she replied, "Dad, dance on Wednesdays has been cancelled for several weeks now! No more competition! Remember? That's why we had time to buy pointe shoes and why we're going to Uncle Peter's for supper."

Juliana heard Dad remove his shoes and then come up the two stairs into the kitchen.

"Right. Okay, no dance. Have you sewed the ribbons and elastics onto your pointe shoes yet?"

Juliana planted her hands on her hips. "Dad! You brought me home an hour ago and pointe class isn't until Monday. I'll look after my shoes on the weekend."

Dad nodded, but his lack of a reaction to her tone of voice suggested he wasn't registering his daughter's frustration. "Have you done your homework?"

"Can you please relax? School's almost over, so it's study time now, and yes, I'm on schedule with my studying."

"Are you sure?"

"Dad!"

Dad looked at his watch, again not appearing to be aware of Juliana's exasperation. "We'll leave in an hour."

He headed for his and Mom's bedroom, muttering reminders to himself.

"Is that what I look like when I'm worried I'm going to forget something?" Opa asked.

The twinkle in Opa's eye told Juliana she could laugh at his question. "But do you see what I'm talking about, Opa? He's Helicopter Dad!"

Opa furrowed his eyebrows together. "I know what a helicopter is, but I don't know what you mean."

"Haven't you heard of helicopter parents? The ones that hover around, protecting you against everything, even a paper cut?"

Now it was Opa's turn to laugh. He sat back down on the couch and Juliana followed suit. "That's very funny," he said. "Once Mammi and I moved back to Semlak—I was still very young—I could run around almost anywhere I wanted to because everyone looked out for everyone. But when Irmgard and I moved to Canada... I think you would call us helicopter parents."

Juliana laughed and shook her head. "There's no way you were this bad. Maybe I'll call him Foreman Roth."

Opa playfully wagged his finger at her. "Be careful what you say, Yulika. Your mother, aunt, and uncle could make their own breakfast, but they had to be home by eight every night, even in high school."

Juliana's jaw dropped. "Eight? In high school?"

"And they were not allowed to join clubs after school. Peter wanted to join the wrestling club, but we wouldn't let him. We didn't want him to get hurt."

"But you let Mom and Aunt Anne dance?"

Opa nodded. "Oma waited in the waiting room every week while they had their lessons, but we knew if we showed up to watch Peter practise his wrestling, his friends would laugh."

"So...you just didn't let him wrestle?"

Opa smiled. "I think you should call me Foreman Opa."

Juliana laughed. "Okay, that is bad. But Dad still has to chill. After all, he's not new to Canada!"

Opa patted her on the shoulder again and smiled. "Just new to being home every evening with you."

Juliana begrudgingly agreed with Opa. But if Dad was acting this way because he was home every night now, then it stood to reason that once he got used to staying home, he would stop.

When would that be? When Juliana graduated from high school?

CHAPTER FOUR

Elisabeth jumped out of bed. "One day closer to Tata's arrival!" she shouted.

All she heard were groans: everyone still lay in their beds in the front room. Elisabeth whipped open the curtain that hung just past her bed. The sun was only now rising. A dream about Tata had awoken her, but now she had disturbed everyone else's sleep.

"Sorry, Jesus," she said quietly, looking toward the crucifix on the wall of the back room.

"Elisabeth," Mammi grumbled. "What do you mean by shouting what we already know?"

Rosina pulled her sheets over her head. Anna's mattress rustled under her as she turned around and buried her head under her pillow. Luki rolled into a ball and did both, burying his head under his pillow and pulling his sheets over everything.

A moment later, Mammi was snoring again.

Too many thoughts whirled in her head, keeping her from falling back to sleep: Exactly when was Tata coming home? His telegram had only said "in August." And why was he coming home? Was he wounded somehow? He worked in a factory and sometimes the weekly news from Temeswar included reports about an accident at a factory in Romania. But if he were wounded, he would come home earlier, wouldn't he? Or were no tickets for passage on a ship available until August? She wanted to ask him so many questions!

Would he bring something home for her? Maybe a new dress? But what would fit? And would it be too short? Those pictures in the magazine Maria's grandmother's cousin had mailed in the winter were filled with photos of women in short dresses. Stefan would never look at her again, and Mammi would throw her out of the house if Elisabeth started walking the streets of Semlak in a dress that only reached to her knees.

To say nothing of Pastor Fröhlich, who would waste no time spreading the news of her shortcomings.

"And Tata would disown me," she said aloud to herself. "All right, then, no dress. Maybe a hat?"

Soft groans from one of her siblings reminded her to

close her mouth, so Elisabeth decided to change in the back room and do her siblings' morning chores so that they would appreciate her early rising.

She gathered the morning's necessities as silently as possible—a washcloth, hairpins, a brush, an old skirt, an apron, a blouse, and a pair of cotton socks that Mammi had knit—and headed to the back room to change.

Hmm...socks. Would Tata want a new pair of socks as a welcome home gift? Would that make him happy?

I should start today, she thought. *It takes me longer to knit a pair of socks than it does for a turtle to pass through Hungary. No, Romania.* Until the end of the war, Semlak had belonged to the Austrian-Hungarian Empire, specifically to the country of Hungary. The empire had fallen after the war, and the following year, in 1919, Semlak became a part of Romania. Six months had since passed, but Elisabeth still found it difficult to remember sometimes, especially because some things hadn't changed: she spoke German to other Germans and Hungarian to anyone in the village who was not German. Pastor Fröhlich still conducted service in Hungarian although all hymns were still sung in German. The most important change Elisabeth had seen so far was in the schools: whereas she had learned Hungarian and German in school, her brother and sister now learned Romanian and German.

Dressed, Elisabeth brushed her hair, starting at the scalp and drawing the brush all the way down. When she reached a section that hung near the front and pulled her wooden brush through it, it landed with a thud on the loam-and-chaff floor. It took her a moment to realize what had happened before she giggled: the news of Tata's return had erased her memory of Maria cutting her bangs yesterday!

She glanced up at the crucifix. "I must admit," she said to Jesus, "I don't know if I like these bangs." She had seen herself in the looking glass yesterday and found the image she saw very odd.

The looking glass hung in the front room, so unfortunately she couldn't inspect her new hair style again right now. She picked up the brush and continued brushing her hair.

"But the rest of my hair looks the same, so the change isn't too much." She reached for a large chunk of hair at the side to braid it. But when she attempted to hold the three strands in her fingers, the hair slipped out. She wasn't used to braiding so little hair along the sides. After a few tries, Elisabeth succeeded: one braid on each side of her head led into one long braid at the back. She pinned the tip in place at the top of her head.

Elisabeth quickly ate a slice of bread with butter, took an empty cup out to the cellar at the back of the house, and served herself some cooled boiled milk. Her family wouldn't wake up for another hour. She couldn't wait to see their faces when she told them they didn't have to do their morning chores.

But she also needed to decide what she could do for Tata that would make him just as happy. Perhaps knitting socks was not the answer. She remembered Maria's idea of planning a celebration.

ALL THREE SIBLINGS gave Elisabeth a big hug and thanked her again for helping with their chores. The instant Anna and Luki left for school, Elisabeth rushed to catch her reflection in the looking glass. She pushed her bangs to the side and looked at the old Elisabeth for a moment. Then she let them fall into place, and looked at the new Elisabeth.

"This is going to take some time to get used to," she said herself.

"Elisabeth, stop staring at yourself and get to work," Mammi said from the kitchen. "You look funny, and the looking glass won't change that. Stefan will be here soon. Do not keep him waiting."

Stefan! In all her rush, Elisabeth had completely forgotten! "Yes, Mammi!"

Normally, Elisabeth would drive herself out to the *salasch*: because of an incident a few months ago with Peter-Bátschi, Mammi's brother, Elisabeth had asked Georg and Stefan to show her how to drive a wagon. Unfortunately, a wheel had broken a few days before when she accidentally drove over a large stone, and the wainwright couldn't come until tomorrow to repair it.

But Elisabeth wasn't going to complain: she thanked Jesus for any change to spend time with Stefan.

A knock on the door signalled his arrival.

Elisabeth held her breath as she patted at her bangs to make sure they were straight. She tucked wisps of hair behind her ears and smoothed her apron. When she opened the door, as much as she had planned to look him straight in the eye as usual, her eyes looked down, her cheeks feeling like they were on fire as she waited to hear his reaction to her new hair style. In the moment of silence that followed, she noticed the scattered holes sewn shut throughout Stefan's loose linen pants. Yes, he was dressed for farming, and one certainly did not wear one's Sunday best, but his pants had been repaired more often than, say, Tata's ever had been. Stefan wore a loose, white cotton shirt, with one sleeve rolled up to just below the elbow and the other cut off and hemmed above the elbow, where Stefan had lost his arm in the war.

Finally, Stefan broke the silence. "Elisabeth? Is everything all right?"

Elisabeth nodded and slowly raised her eyes to meet his from under the wide-brimmed straw hat he wore to help protect him from the sun. His eyes were wide open as he looked at her hair, and Elisabeth covered her forehead.

"You don't like it?"

To her surprise, Stefan burst out laughing. "Is that what you're so worried about?"

She nodded again. Stefan shook his head in disbelief. "I thought something terrible had happened."

Elisabeth gasped as her hands flew to her chest. "Oh, no, Stefan! Not at all! I'm so very sorry!"

Stefan offered his arm, which Elisabeth took gladly.

"Lissika!" Mammi called from the back room. "You sit far away from him! I will hear about anything forbidden before you return home!"

Did Mammi really think Elisabeth would do anything that would embarrass her family? What kind of a woman did Mammi take Elisabeth for? But Elisabeth knew better than to share her thoughts with her mother. *Honour thy mother and father*, she thought. *You make that really hard sometimes, God.*

"I will behave, Mammi, I promise."

Mammi wagged a finger at Elisabeth, and Elisabeth's cheeks turned red again. Once outside, Elisabeth muttered, "I'm not a child anymore."

Stefan chuckled. "Frau Schuhmacher just worries about her oldest daughter, that's all."

Stefan might find Mammi's reminder funny, but Elisabeth certainly did not. She sighed. "I'd better sit in the wagon and let you drive," she said.

Elisabeth knew Stefan would never act rudely toward her. She would have preferred to join him on the bench at the front of the wagon while he drove simply because sitting together made talking much easier. But risking family embarrassment and possible punishment from Mammi, no matter the actual truth, was not worth it.

Stefan helped Elisabeth over the back of the wagon and she sat as close to the front as possible. He climbed onto the bench at the front, and before he gave the reins a snap, turned to Elisabeth and gave her a gentle smile. She returned it, not only because she liked him but because he liked her bangs.

That was one thing less to worry about!

AFTER SPENDING the day hoeing weeds in the fields, Elisabeth's arms ached. But the sun still shone after supper, and so she sat with Mammi, Anna, and Rosina behind the house in their small summer kitchen, each one working on a project: Anna was adding embroidery embellishments to an everyday blouse Elisabeth had passed down to her. Rosina was knitting a scarf she had begun at Christmas. Elisabeth worked on hemming a skirt for Rosina that had once belonged to her and then Anna. Elisabeth always got newly sewed clothing, Luki sometimes received new clothing and other times hand-me-downs from family, while Anna made do with hand-me-downs, and poor Rosina was stuck with only old pieces whose hems and seams would be once again let out as she grew.

Perhaps Tata should bring a new dress home for her, Elisabeth thought.

Luki tended to the lone horse they kept on their property and whose stall stood behind the summer kitchen, separated by a wall and covered by a thatch roof. The other horse was at the *salasch*, where Georg's brother and sister-in-law took care of it.

With Mammi focused on her embroidery, now was a good time to ask about Maria's idea.

"With Tata returning in two months, I would like to have a celebration for him to welcome him home. What do you think, Mammi?"

Before Mammi could answer, Rosina offered her idea. "You have to have lots of pickles and cheese and bread and sausage and *kipfel*!"

Kipfel were small crescent-shaped cookies made with flour, almond meal, sugar, and butter, and dusted with powdered sugar before serving. Elisabeth loved eating them but disliked baking them because of all the rolling.

"When do you have the time to plan something?" Mammi never once lifted her gaze from the upper of a pair of silk house shoes she was embroidering. "He's just your father. Let him come home and rest."

Luki came out of the horse stalls, dusting the hay from his linen pants. "You must also have schnapps."

Hearing such an adult suggestion from a young boy made Elisabeth laugh in a loving kind of way, but her laugh prompted a scowl from Luki.

Anna laid her embroidery on her lap. "I think we should have something small, just with close family."

"But who would that be?" Elisabeth asked. "Both Mammi and Tata's families are large." Although Tata only had one brother, Konrad-Bátschi and Margarethe-Néni had four grown children, all of whom were married. Mammi had one surviving brother and two sisters, and they all had children, too, though in a variety of ages. Their mother, whom Elisabeth and her siblings called Omama, lived with Mammi's brother and his family.

"Georg and Eva, Samuel and Deaf-Lissi. And Stefan. They're nice people and they're close family," Anna said.

Elisabeth blushed—Stefan was technically not family, but he had helped out on their property from time to time, and the children had grown fond of him. Anna often solved any problem by providing a logical answer: she only wanted to have people over whose company she enjoyed, and they happened to be "close family."

She couldn't blame her sister, either. When Anna had first seen one of Georg's fits, she had also caught sight of Margarethe-Néni slapping him to make him stop so he would no longer embarrass the family. Sometime later, as winter was turning into spring, Elisabeth had witnessed Konrad-Bátschi beat Georg in public for the same reason. It made sense that Anna didn't want her aunt and uncle present.

Mammi clucked her tongue at Anna. "That's not how we treat family. If we invite family, we invite all of Tata's family, whether we like them or not." Mammi never hid her dislike of Tata's brother and sister-in-law, but she always did her duty. Mammi's side was perhaps not as cruel as Tata's family, but it was not much better.

"But Lissika has never planned a big celebration before," Anna said. "Isn't it like embroidering? You start with something small and once you're good at it, you can try something bigger?"

Mammi paused her work and turned her attention to Elisabeth. "Your sister is right. You must plan something small. You have never hosted a large gathering before. Therefore invite perhaps only your father's family. But whatever you decide, I cannot help you. I have more orders for women's embroidered house shoes and dress shoes with heels than God has angels." Elisabeth nodded. "And do not think that because I am so busy, we have money to spend on frivolous trinkets and expensive food. At most, you may buy Tata coffee that he can enjoy when he returns, but no tea or coffee for the guests. They are family. They know our situation, and we will have dried chamomile and peppermint from this year's garden. But whatever you plan, you must do it yourself."

Elisabeth took a deep breath and nodded. She wanted to show Tata how much she had missed him—and help her siblings show him that, too. This celebration had to be very special.

CHAPTER FIVE

Opa, Juliana, and her parents walked to Uncle Peter's condo in Waterloo, Kitchener's twin city. Juliana had protested Dad's plan at first—walking, she had argued, wasn't as efficient as driving. Dad had replied that it was indeed much more efficient than driving and that only cycling would have been more efficient than walking. Juliana tried not to roll her eyes, but a disapproving look from Mom told her she hadn't quite concealed the eye roll. But she was trying, she really was!

She also had to admit that the nice trail that led from her neighbourhood to Uptown Waterloo and Uncle Peter's condo actually wasn't that bad. Lots of bushes and trees were covered in new green leaves, while unfamiliar wild-flowers stuck up from the ground in between. Some of the longer stretches even inspired a travelling tap combination in her head. Too bad the asphalt would wreck her tap shoes.

Opa told her that the trail had replaced an old railroad, and a spur line of the railway had connected the train with the factory. "You could hear the train rumble at night, because it passed right where that ramp is to Belmont Village."

Juliana was a bit surprised: that rail line was indeed very close to Opa's house!

Once they got to Uncle Peter's condo, Sophie whipped open the door. "Now you're three years older than me," she declared, "but that doesn't give you an excuse to treat me like a kid."

Juliana swatted her cousin in the arm. "I couldn't treat you like a kid if I wanted to! Besides, you turn thirteen later this year. That's hardly a kid anymore!"

Uncle Peter flashed his famous cheesy smile. "That's because little Sophie would get you back."

"I'm not little!" Sophie paid the swat forward and hit their uncle in the upper arm. Laughing, Uncle Peter backed away, holding his hands up in surrender.

"Peter!" Mom admonished her younger brother. "That's not how you treat your niece at her birthday celebration!"

But the mischief in Uncle Peter's eyes shone like the sun, and Juliana could never be angry at him. If anything, she regretted not knowing him sooner. His happy personality, blond mullet, and what Juliana would call almost devotional love to the Eighties—highlighted by the Eighties music station playing in the background—made her uncle the dream uncle every kid wanted.

However, once Mom, Dad, Opa, and Sophie had left the foyer to sit at the dining room table, Uncle Peter took Juliana aside and beckoned to Brian, his partner, to come over. Was Juliana about to be the recipient of some silly joke? Or was she about to get in trouble? She was certain she hadn't done anything wrong. But when you're a teen, sometimes it feels like you can't do anything right.

Uncle Peter and Brian held hands.

"You have to promise us," Uncle Peter said, "to not make a sound."

Juliana's gaze went back and forth between the two men.

Brian added, "Pete said you might squeal. Literally. Promise?"

Juliana's heart thumped wildly. The corners of their mouths were fighting to stay straight and not curl up. Were they going to share good news with her? Before everyone else? How could she not squeal? She wore her emotions on her sleeve! But she nodded.

Uncle Peter smiled. "We really don't want to crash your party. It's your first birthday in Kitchener...we know it's special. But Opa's memory is slipping, and there's something we want to tell everyone."

Juliana covered her mouth with both hands, and Uncle

Peter glanced over his shoulder to make sure no one else was listening.

He lowered his voice. "Do you mind if after the cake we announce our engagement?"

Don't squeal! Juliana pressed her hands against her mouth to keep her joy from bursting out. She nodded an exuberant yes, and then shook her head to say no, meaning no, she didn't mind, not yes, she did mind. But she meant yes, they could make the announcement. Did they understand her?

Brian wrapped his arms around her. "Thank you!" he whispered. "We hope the earlier we tell Opa, the better his chances of remembering later."

Juliana pressed her lips shut as she hugged Uncle Peter back.

"We would have told you sooner instead of cornering you here," Brian continued, "but your uncle warned me that if we told you before you came, you'd be dancing around your house and everyone would guess something was up."

Juliana shrugged. "What can I say? He knows me really well!"

With Aunt Anne and Uncle Phillip's entire clan there, food seemed to take forever to get passed around. When it reached Juliana, she threw food on her plate and passed the bowls of food to Sophie so fast she almost made her cousin drop it.

Dinner couldn't go fast enough for Juliana, who shovelled her food despite Dad's frequent reminders to slow down. He even knew useless facts about efficient digestion! Mom scolded him a few times, but he didn't listen.

Juliana disappeared to the bathroom a couple of times —prompting questions of concern about the food from Aunt Anne, who had done most of the cooking—but she needed somewhere to shake out the giddiness without tipping anyone off. *My tap board would be very useful right now!* she thought. When Uncle Phillip asked about her excitement, she blamed her first birthday in Kitchener. When that didn't seem to be enough and Sophie asked more questions, she blamed her pointe shoe shopping experience with Dad. That it made her happy wasn't true, but she was glad to have new shoes, and she had to say something or her anticipation of the announcement might make her explode. It didn't matter if she was angry or excited: Juliana couldn't hide her emotions. That sometimes made her a terrible liar, which was occasionally a problem.

By the time the dinner dishes were clear—but before the birthday cake arrived—Juliana announced that Uncle Peter and Brian had something to say. The table fell silent as everyone stared at the two men.

Uncle Peter shook his head, laughing, as he and Brian stood up. Uncle Peter ruffled Juliana's hair. "I was right, wasn't I, Brian? Juliana can't keep a secret, even for ninety minutes."

"You were right, but I'll never admit that again."

Uncle Peter explained that they had asked Juliana's permission to make an announcement during her birthday celebration.

He and Brian held hands, exchanged glances, took a deep breath, and then spoke in unison: "We're getting married!"

Both men pulled engagement rings from their pant pockets and placed them on each other's fingers while the entire Schuhmacher clan broke out in cheers.

Aunt Anne and Mom sprang out of their chairs at the same time and playfully fought who got to hug Uncle Peter first.

"Don't I count?" Brian said.

Within moments, all twelve family members were hugging the newly engaged couple.

"Okay," Mom said, "I do have to ask. What last name are you going with? Schuhmacher? Yamamoto? Schuhmacher-Yamamoto? Yamamoto-Schuhmacher?"

Both men smiled at each other, and Juliana was afraid they'd kiss before answering Mom. She couldn't stand it when adults kissed in public. It was just gross.

Brian answered. "I think we'll keep our separate names, but to be honest—"

"We haven't really talked about it all too much," Uncle

Peter finished.

Mom hugged the men again. "Well, whatever it is, I am so happy for you both."

Once everyone sat down, Opa clinked his glass with a spoon and stood up, his face sombre. The room fell as silent as a theatre before the curtain opens.

Opa raised his glass, which only had water in it because of his medication. His voice cracked as he spoke. "I am so grateful for all the memories—" He swallowed and started again. "I am so grateful for all the memories I have of Peter working with me in the factory. We had many happy summers. I know that he became an industrial engineer because of that." Opa's eyes began to turn red. "But I must be honest. When Peter was younger and told me and Irmgard that he liked men...we were not good parents."

Opa pulled a handkerchief out of his pocket and dried his eyes. Juliana blinked tears out of her own eyes and others around the table did the same. Only Scott, who was just eight years old, looked bored, but Juliana knew it was because he didn't understand what was happening.

Opa swallowed and made eye contact with Uncle Peter, who already had a tissue in one hand and was holding Brian's hand tightly with the other. "I'm sure your mother is here right now, and before anyone thinks I'm seeing things again, I am not. I'm sure she's here now and wishes you could hear her say this, too." Opa paused, collecting his thoughts.

Mom had told Juliana a few months ago that Opa and Oma had wanted Uncle Peter to change when he came out, to like women instead of men. Mom, and later Uncle Peter, had emphasized that Opa had changed his opinions a long time ago and now accepted Uncle Peter as he was. If Opa said anything mean about Uncle Peter, it was his dementia speaking, not Opa.

"I think my memory is good tonight," Opa continued. "I remember showing you the factory and teasing you when you said you liked the second, newer factory better after ours closed and we were transferred. I remember when you later showed me floor plans from factories you designed and told me why they were even better than both of our factories." Opa nodded. "Yes, I remember all these things tonight from that time, and they made me and your *modr* proud to be your parents. But we were not proud of how we treated you. You were honest with us, and I know that was very hard. Your mother and I were not nice to you. My memories are good tonight, and I don't remember that we ever asked you for forgiveness for that."

Juliana had never experienced such a deep silence before in her family. Despite the tears and downward gazes, she somehow sensed that no one was truly sad. Instead, it was like the moment you finished a dance and knew that everything had assembled itself together into something magical and beautiful: the team, the emotion, the steps. Everything. In that moment, when the dance was done, there was a release of energy, an acknowledgement of connection and wonder. Often, many on the team cried, but it was out of...happiness wasn't the right word. It was neither that light nor fleeting. It was joy. They cried because of the joy they felt together, created by the hard work and dedication each member of the team contributed to the dance. In that moment, the team understood what it meant to feel unified in purpose and task, and that release celebrated that feeling.

That was what Juliana was sensing right now.

"Tata, it doesn't matter anymore," Uncle Peter said, his own face streaked with tears. His and Brian's hands were still tightly clasped together.

"Yes, it does, my son. I'm asking for me and also for your mother. Will you forgive us?"

Uncle Peter let go of Brian's hand. "Of course."

Sophie tried to wipe her face with her sleeve, but she needed a tissue or something. She touched her hand around her plate. "Where's my napkin?" she whispered to Juliana. Sophie was losing her eyesight in the centre of her vision, which made it hard to see anything directly in front of her. With the napkins and tablecloth being white, Juliana imagined it was probably hard to see anything.

"Actually, it fell on the floor. I'll get it for you."

When Juliana sat up straight again, Uncle Peter and Opa were in a tight embrace.

CHAPTER SIX

It was a cloudy Monday morning as Elisabeth rode her wagon, its wheel now fixed, to the store. The distance was not far—she usually walked. But today she needed sugar and yeast for baking, and gasoline for their lanterns. Afterwards, she was to go to the tanner to pick up Mammi's order for leather. It was simply easier to load the items into the wagon than it was to carry them home or make several trips, and it was easier to do it herself rather than get a man in the family to help. Mammi didn't like Georg helping unless it was necessary, and Peter-Bátschi had proven unreliable to Elisabeth and her family in the past.

Anna was right: Elisabeth had never planned a large celebration before. If she invited all of Tata's and Mammi's families, it would be busier than last Christmas, when only Mammi's family had come, and back then, Mammi had looked after everything and ordered her four children about. No one disobeyed her unless they wanted to kneel in dried corn kernels in front of all the guests. In her heart, Elisabeth didn't believe Jesus would want her to physically punish her siblings in that way. But she didn't know how to make them listen to her all the time either.

She tugged gently on the right rein and turned the corner onto the main street.

But if she was the only reliable person available to plan this gathering, it would have to be very small. Who could she invite without insulting others?

No, she would invite many people—Tata deserved it!—and would therefore need help, and she saw just the person walking ahead of her on the road.

Elisabeth called out to Maria, who turned around and waved. A few moments later, Elisabeth halted the horse so her best friend could climb onto the wagon's bench beside her. Maria was all smiles, her eyes full of anticipation.

"So?"

Elisabeth understood what she was asking about: if Stefan had approved of her bangs and was therefore still interested in her. She blushed. "He said he liked them."

"See! I was right!"

Elisabeth laughed as she tapped Maria with the reins. "You didn't even know if he would!"

Maria waved Elisabeth's accusation away. "It doesn't matter. The important thing is that he liked them."

Elisabeth smiled as she snapped the reins and the horse continued on its way.

"I still can't believe your mother allows you to drive a wagon," Maria said.

"Mammi didn't want Georg helping us all the time, so it was a simple decision for her."

"But you do understand why your mother feels as she does, don't you? Why almost everyone in the community feels that way? Georg was so mean all those years. He even insisted that your Adam-Bátschi wasn't enough of a man to stay alive during the war. What does that say about him not protecting your Andreas-Bátschi?"

Elisabeth pressed her lips together to push her anger down. Stefan had told her why Georg couldn't protect Mammi's brother on the front, but was she allowed to tell that story? Would it even matter? Mammi didn't believe it. But Maria wasn't Mammi: she was her best friend.

"That's not the whole story."

Maria shrugged. "What else is there to know? Georg promised to bring your Andreas-Bátschi home. Instead, Georg came home, and your uncle died on the front. A man keeps his promises. Georg did not."

The gravel crackled under the wheels as Elisabeth took a deep breath to calm herself. This was not the conversation Elisabeth had hoped for. But Maria was a dear friend, so, unlike most others in their church, she meant no malice when she said such things. The question—no, the accusation—bothered Elisabeth nonetheless. *But You were patient with people*, she silently said to Jesus. *I must try to be patient, too.* She took one more breath. She had heard this accusation so often that to respond to it properly, like a woman, took strength.

"Georg was...a horrible person before the war," Elisabeth said. Sharing her honest feelings about her cousin was difficult because the war had changed him so much. It hardly seemed fair to speak ill of him. But she also wanted to show Maria she understood. "We both know that. He used to pull my hair all the time when I was a child, and I would often run out of the room when he came in. He punched kids on the way home from school even after he was finished with school. He told my father not to marry my mother."

Elisabeth pulled on the reins to slow the horse as they neared the dry goods store. "But Georg could not protect Mammi's brother in the war as he had promised because their commanding officer split them up before they attacked. Stefan told me that Georg searched for Andreas-Bátschi among the wounded in the field hospital, but when he saw him, he knew my uncle would die soon. He won't tell me more details than that."

Maria gasped. "Is that really the truth?"

Elisabeth commanded the horse to stop. She rested her

hands, still holding the reins in her lap, and faced her best friend. "If you disobeyed your commanding officer, he could shoot you. What was Georg supposed to do?"

The young women climbed down from the wagon and Elisabeth tied the reins to a tree outside the store.

Maria patted the horse's mane, her eyes staring at the ground, her voice barely above a whisper. "I didn't know that. That's horrible."

The conversation had become too sad when Elisabeth had been feeling so ecstatic about Tata's return. She didn't want to leave her best friend or herself in such a mood. She grabbed Maria's hands and let her excitement from before shine through. They could talk more about Georg later, if Maria wanted to.

"Listen. I want to plan a welcome home celebration for Tata, but I've never done this before on my own. Should I even try?"

As Elisabeth explained her concerns about hosting such a celebration, Maria's eyes brightened and the corners of her mouth turned up in a smile. When Elisabeth finished, Maria clapped her hands with joy. "I would love to help you with your celebration! I'm sure your sisters would, too!"

Elisabeth shrugged. "I'm honestly not sure. Sometimes they listen to me, and sometimes they don't. I'm hoping that if I have a good friend to help me, Anna and Rosina will want to join in. But how much food do I need? How much do I bake? What time should I offer it? And how can I enjoy spending time with Tata at his celebration if I'm running around serving everyone?"

Elisabeth walked toward the dry goods store, Maria following her inside. After they exchanged greetings with the shopkeeper, Elisabeth gave him her order and he collected the items. The shopkeeper and his wife belonged to a handful of Germans in the village who were Catholics. They had come from across the Marosch River, in Perjamosch, and settled here.

"I have an idea," Maria said. "What if you started small, like Anna suggested, but not for your father's celebration? You have two months. What if you hosted a few *majen* evenings? Maybe the first one in a week or two? I would definitely help you with all of them if you wanted me to! After a little practice, you'll feel more comfortable having more guests over for your father."

Elisabeth had attended a few evenings of *majen* already. They were small gatherings of young women at which everyone would work on their handicrafts while they gossiped. Often, a respected older woman in the community would teach those gathered a new technique. Although Elisabeth disliked the gossip, she did enjoy talking to others her age and older.

Hosting a few *majen* evenings sounded perfect.

Elisabeth wrapped her arms around her best friend in a big hug. "Yes! Let's do it!"

After Elisabeth paid for her wares, the young women decided to meet at Elisabeth's house after lunch to plan for an evening of *majen*.

But before they parted, Maria became solemn again. "While you were waiting for the shopkeeper, I had time to think about your cousin. I pity him for being forced to leave your uncle. If someone made me do that to you, I'd carry that pain with me for the rest of my life."

Elisabeth gave her friend another tight hug. "And so would I. But let's not worry about that right now. I think the reason Georg and Stefan don't tell me much about the war is because they don't want me to be sad so often."

Maria smiled. "I've told you before that I don't think Stefan is a good man to marry. I thought having only one arm would make it hard for him to do work around your home. But he cares for you and respects you. That is so important." Maria kissed Elisabeth on both cheeks. "We will have fun this afternoon planning your first *majen*." She did a quick jump and turned to go on her way, leaving Elisabeth with happy thoughts about her first social gathering *and* Stefan.

But she couldn't deny that what gave her more happiness than either of those thoughts was that Maria had clearly opened her heart just a little to Georg.

CHAPTER SEVEN

"That's awesome news, isn't it?" Sophie asked Juliana as they sat on the sofa in the entertainment area of Uncle Peter's condo, waiting for the birthday cake to be served. "But you knew, didn't you?"

Juliana clapped her hands to her cheeks. "I couldn't keep it in anymore! They wanted to wait until after the cake because the point of this evening was my birthday, which is great, but with Opa's memory slipping, they wanted to tell everyone in front of Opa as soon as possible."

Sophie giggled. "You were so wiggly!"

Juliana smiled at the comment. "I couldn't keep it inside! But when Opa asked Uncle Peter for forgiveness..." Her voice trailed off.

"That silence, right? I don't think I've ever felt like that before."

"It was beautiful, wasn't it?"

"It was acceptance."

Uncle Peter approached them.

"Hey, Jules! Sophie!" He held a manila envelope in his hands, and both girls jumped off the sofa and hugged him.

"That's so awesome you're getting married!" Juliana said.

"Totally!" Sophie added. "Can I be the flower girl?"

Juliana raised an eyebrow. "Aren't you a little old?"

Sophie shrugged. "I'm also the youngest girl in the family."

"Then who am I going to be a bridesmaid with?" Her hand flew to her mouth. "Wait. Will you have only groomsmen then? Or, um..." Her cheeks flashed hotter than after an hour of intense dance.

Uncle Peter's flashy smile looked even flashier, if that was possible. "Don't worry, Juliana. Once we have details worked out, you'll be the first to know. Trust me, our wedding will be awesome, and we hope all our close family members can help." He leaned into them. "I was thinking about getting Brian to take dance lessons with me and we'll learn one of the *Dirty Dancing* dances."

Juliana and Sophie wrinkled their noses. That was definitely too much info. She did not want to see her uncle and fiancé dirty dancing.

Uncle Peter broke into his jolly laughter again. "It's a movie. You know, with Patrick Swayze?"

Both girls shook their heads.

Uncle Peter sighed. "Youth these days. Your parents don't educate you. But guess what else is awesome? My employer changed my job so I don't have to travel so much anymore."

Sophie's face lit up like a Christmas tree. Juliana was happy, too, but she didn't know their uncle as well as Sophie did.

"At least you don't have kids at home to badger, like *some* fathers I know." Juliana had meant the comment as a joke, but no sooner had she said it than she realized she'd expressed her true feelings.

Uncle Peter glanced at Dad, who was chatting with Brian and Uncle Phillip at the dining table. "Annie was telling me about Foreman Roth."

"Uncle Peter, you have *no* idea." Juliana told him about his nagging at breakfast, the pointe shoe shopping trip this afternoon, and Dad's panicked entrance an hour before they had to leave. Uncle Peter and Sophie laughed harder at each story. "He's driving me absolutely crazy! Yes, I wanted him home but not without the time travel to when I was a little kid."

Uncle Peter wiped the tears from his eyes as he calmed down. "Yeah, I get that. Give him time to come around. I'm sure I'll start driving Brian crazy, too, once he moves in here." Uncle Peter opened the envelope. "Speaking of time travel, I found something that might interest you. I came across these while I was clearing out more space for his stuff."

He pulled out several photos and handed them to Juliana.

"These are from when Tata and I worked in the rubber factory together."

Juliana's eyes grew wide and she forgot that Sophie might not have been able to see the photos well. Anything about her family's past hijacked her brain.

Uncle Peter pointed to the photo on top. "That's me—"

Juliana snorted. "You've had a mullet that long?" Sophie laughed, too.

"Hey, it looked good on me!" Uncle Peter looked back at the photo. "We're standing in front of a Banbury. That was used to mix the rubber."

"Was the work that dirty?" Both Opa and Uncle Peter looked like they'd spent a day cleaning chimneys.

"That's the carbon black. Really not healthy stuff. We got changed at work so we wouldn't bring that crap home. It's been in the news lately. Not sure if you've heard?"

Juliana remembered when the news had reported increased cancer cases among former workers at the factory. Karl, Opa's best friend from work, had been diagnosed with cancer several years before. He was now in remission, but Opa said Karl worried a lot about it returning. Juliana worried Opa would become sick with cancer, too.

Sophie tucked her hands into her pockets and stared at the floor. "Will you get sick from it?"

Uncle Peter laid his hand on Sophie's shoulder. "I only worked in those factories in the summers and only for six years. Besides, by the time I started, the company had introduced personal protective equipment and such. The old-timers fought tooth and nail to not use it—it slowed them down. But I used it. That's still no guarantee, but Tata said that many of the men who've died so far were lifers, like him, and worked in the earlier decades, when the only equipment you might have had supplied was a pair of overalls."

"But don't you work in factories now?"

"I do, but I design mostly food processing plants. I don't think I've designed a rubber factory in over a decade, and the safety measures nowadays are extremely detailed and regulated. Back when Opa started, no one cared."

"They probably weren't aware of it either," Juliana offered. One thing she was learning through Opa and his stories about his mother was that sometimes bad things happened simply because people didn't know any better.

But Uncle Peter shook his head. "Maybe in the Seventies they didn't, but they knew in the Eighties for sure. The companies just didn't want to do anything about it." After a quiet pause, he continued. "But that's not why I wanted to show you these. I have so many happy memories with Tata precisely because of them. I thought this might help you and your dad—"

They looked back to her father again, but now he was talking with Mom, his voice raised and agitated, and they could hear the conversation.

Uncle Peter furrowed his brow after Mom and Dad stopped talking. "He wants you to leave now...before the birthday cake...to go to bed?" He glanced at his watch. "It's not even eight-thirty."

"See what I mean?" She grabbed her uncle and cousin by the arm. "The two of you have to help me! You're a man. You can tell me how men think." She turned to Sophie. "And your dad's normal. You must have ideas!"

"But I'm less knowledgeable about how *dads* think," Uncle Peter said. He switched to another photo. "But here's why I wanted to give these to you. You can't work alongside your dad at his job—"

Juliana interjected. "Actually, when I was younger and we lived in Calgary, I joined him on some of his trips. Just the day ones, but it was nice."

Sophie's eyes sparkled. "*That* must have been fun!"

Juliana nodded. "It was—I got to hang out in the sleeper part, and we ate truck-stop food and would drive through the Rockies sometimes. It was amazing."

"That does sound like fun," Uncle Peter said. "Annie said Paul's taking some college courses. You're an excellent student. Why don't you help him study? I'm sure that's nowhere near as exciting as riding in his truck, but it would let you spend time with him. Or see if he wants to go out for coffee—or tea, or whatever you drink. Something like that might help him relax a bit. Even when Tata and I didn't see eye to eye on...on some things...we could still build our relationship."

"Yeah!" Sophie added. "You're super organized, Juliana. You could plan some time together with him."

A word Sophie said clicked in Juliana's head. "Plan! That's right! I need a plan. Opa said I have to be patient, but you two just saw what I'm up against. I can't wait this out. I'll be grey and balding by the time Dad relaxes. I need a plan..."

Uncle Peter pointed to Sophie. "You must have some tips, don't you, Sophie?"

Sophie shrugged. "I don't know. I kind of hide behind my siblings and let them take the blame."

Uncle Peter clucked his tongue. "Sophie! I never thought *you* would do that."

Sophie crossed her arms. "Oh, please. Like you never did?"

These were the moments that made Juliana still feel like an outsider. The ease with which Sophie and Uncle Peter jibed with each other was something she hadn't grown up with. It wasn't that she and her parents never teased each other, but it wasn't the same. And in the months leading up to the move, anger was the only emotion Juliana had been capable of. Juliana missed Calgary, but now that she saw what she had missed out on all the years she lived out there, she wished her parents had moved to Kitchener sooner.

Uncle Peter feigned an embarrassed laugh. "And, well, um, let's look at the next photo, shall we? Have you met Karl, Juliana?"

He held a black-and-white picture in front of her. A young Opa, standing straight and with a head full of hair, stood next to the man she assumed was Karl—Juliana had never met him, but she remembered seeing him in the news a couple of months ago, talking about his cancer and his work in the factories. There was a third man in the photo standing next to Karl. He looked much older and wore a fedora hat and had a cigarette hanging out of his mouth. But unlike Opa and Karl, who smiled for the camera, this man's face carried so much sadness.

And despite his age and hunched shoulders, he was larger than Opa and Karl. *A large man next to a small woman,* that's how Opa had described Georg in Elisabeth's drawings, because Eva was much shorter than Georg.

Juliana yanked the photo out of her uncle's hand and brought it closer to her face. There were lots of tall men in the world, of course, so this might be wishful thinking. But she saw some similarities between this old man and the younger Georg Elisabeth often drew in her sketchbook.

Could this be Georg? She was certain of it. Except for the fact that it was implausible.

"You don't recognize Karl?" Uncle Peter guessed. "Or you do and he's really handsome in a 1970s kind of way and you want to pin him up?"

Juliana registered her uncle's joke and Sophie's laugh, but her mind had focused on the photo. Not even thinking, she rushed over to Opa.

"Opa, is that Georg?"

Opa's smile vanished in an instant when he saw the picture. "Where did you get this?"

His angry tone took Juliana aback.

"Tata?" Mom asked.

Juliana answered Opa's question. "Um, Uncle Peter was showing me photos from when the two of you worked at the factory."

Opa turned his head away from Juliana. "I don't know who that is."

Opa had acted like this before: if he didn't want to talk about something, he didn't say so outright. Instead, he ignored the topic altogether. But it still hurt Juliana to see him happy and loving one moment and then angry and disapproving the next. She tried to tell herself that it was his dementia, but that didn't make it any easier.

At that moment, Aunt Anne came from the kitchen carrying the birthday cake and led everyone in singing "Happy Birthday" to Juliana. By the time the song was over,

Opa's mood had lifted and he had returned to his jolly self. As he gave Juliana a hug, she slid the photo of Opa, Karl, and possibly Georg into her back pocket.

In her exuberance, she had forgotten that Opa despised Georg. He had called him a poor father and "not a man" in the past. Juliana would compare the photo to an actual one she had at home, plus Elisabeth's drawings of Georg, just to be sure. But every bone in her body told her she was right.

And if she was, what was Georg doing in Kitchener?

Sophie held the door open for Juliana. "Did you go to bed at eight-thirty last night?" She giggled.

Juliana shot her a look as she walked into their favourite haunt, a 1950s-style diner in Belmont Village.

Belmont Village was not actually a village but the name of a short shopping strip in Kitchener. Mom and Aunt Anne had worked at different restaurants and stores there in their teens, and it was a stone's throw away from the rubber factory where Opa and sometimes Uncle Peter had worked. Casimiro, the owner, had known several generations of Schuhmachers, including Juliana's grandparents.

As the girls sat down at a table away from the window, Juliana thanked Sophie for joining her for this emergency meeting.

"It started again this morning! Dad was on my case to

eat slower, wear shorts that hang down to my ankles, and I swear he would've asked me to put my hair in a bun and cover it with a bonnet if I hadn't escaped to the bathroom! And then when I grabbed the door with my right hand to leave, he said it would be more efficient to grab it with my left!"

Sophie laughed. "That sounds hilarious!"

Juliana answered in a flat voice, "It so is not hilarious."

Sophie apologized, still laughing.

Casimiro came over and took their order: strawberry flan and water for Juliana, and a root beer float for Sophie.

Juliana's phone dinged.

Eat healthfully at Casimiro's.

"Healthfully?" she asked Sophie. "Who says 'healthfully' besides my dad?!" Juliana leaned her elbows on the table and folded her hands under her chin. "This is dead serious. Tell me about Uncle Phillip. How does your dad treat you? I need some ideas before I die of a rebellious junk food binge."

Sophie laughed and shrugged. "I have no idea what to tell you. Dad nags me to finish my homework, clean my room, and be nice to Rebecca even when she's mean to me. I don't think that's what you're looking for."

Rebecca was Sophie's older sister—*much* older sister. She was twenty-four. Rebecca was also Sophie's only sister. Sophie's older brothers bugged her in the usual ways, like not putting down the toilet seat, messing her hair, or just ignoring her, but Rebecca seemed to believe it was her job to teach Sophie to speak up for herself as she lost her vision. Her tactics downright embarrassed Sophie—Juliana could tell by her cousin's red cheeks or averted gaze—at family gatherings. Juliana could only imagine what happened when they were at home without guests.

Sophie interrupted Juliana's thoughts. "But now that I think of it, I'd say my dad is more chill than yours. For starters, he doesn't nag me about the length of my shorts."

Casimiro brought over their order, and the girls thanked him.

Sophie lifted her tall glass to her mouth. "It's like your dad doesn't know how to be a work-in-town dad." She took her first sip of her sweet drink out of the straw, closing her eyes in obvious enjoyment.

Juliana pointed at Sophie. "Opa said the same thing."

Sophie sipped on her float. "And Uncle Peter worked with him in the summers once he was old enough. It was always like that. That's what Mom says, anyway."

Julianna enjoyed the cakes at the café. Casimiro's wife baked them. They were sweet but not sting-your-teeth sweet. With strawberries now in season, though, her dessert was divine.

"You know," Juliana said as she chewed, "maybe Dad needs a support group of some kind. Uncle Peter doesn't have any kids, and your dad has six, so neither has ever hovered, which means Dad has no one in the family here to talk to."

"It's like you have to train him—"

Juliana slapped her hand on the table. "That's it! You've got it, Sophie! I have to *train* Dad!"

Sophie's eyes filled with mischief. "'How to Train Your Father.' I like it."

Juliana pulled out her phone from her purse, opened up her voice memo app, and began recording. "First idea, he needs an instruction book."

Sophie sat up straight. "We should check out that bookstore down the street. They must have something."

"Perfect. Buy Dad parenting book."

The girls brainstormed for another hour about all the different ways Juliana could begin training her father to leave her alone. Once Juliana got home, she replayed it and wrote all their good ideas onto a pad of paper. With Sophie's help, she could make a plan to train her father.

And with any luck, he'd finally learn how to parent a teen without acting like a helicopter.

CHAPTER EIGHT

Rain had begun, so Elisabeth set up the table in the summer kitchen where she and Maria could discard the pods from the harvested peas in one basket and collect the individual peas in a glass jar. Elisabeth would feed the pods to the pigs later.

"If you're going to host a *majen* evening next week," Maria said, "we should decide on what you'd like to do."

Elisabeth agreed, but too many thoughts ran through her head: would she bake a beautiful cake or offer cookies? Or bread, butter, cheese, smoked sausage, and pickles? Offering tea and coffee would make the evening very special, but Mammi had forbidden both.

Most importantly, who would she invite to her first evening of *majen*?

"Why don't we look at the Bible?" Elisabeth suggested. "There are many stories about celebrations in it."

Maria liked the idea. They packed everything into their two baskets and headed into the kitchen, staying dry thanks to the overhang that extended from the house's roof.

Elisabeth poured water from the jug into the porcelain washing basin, and both cleaned their hands using a bar of homemade soap. She invited Maria to sit down at the wooden table in the centre of the front room while she got the family Bible from the back room.

"Would you like something to eat?" she called through the house.

"No, thank you, Lissika. I ate well at lunch."

The Bible had been passed down through several generations. Tata had always said that the nice thing about Lutherans was that their Bible was in German. He didn't understand why Catholics had to learn Latin in school. They only used Latin for their church service on Sundays and reading the Bible at home. Elisabeth couldn't imagine spending more time in class to learn a language no one spoke when you could be in the fields or carrying out chores.

She set the heavy, leather-bound book on the table. "Can you think of any feasts?"

"I suppose the Last Supper comes to mind," Maria offered.

Elisabeth searched for it in the New Testament. They skimmed the passage in Matthew and then in Luke.

"It doesn't say exactly what they ate for Passover," Elisabeth said.

Maria peered at the passage in Luke again. "It only says unleavened bread and wine. Oh—and a lamb. We can't serve wine to the guests: they're all women. And everyone would look funny at us—at you!—if you didn't add yeast to the bread."

"We have no idea how to cook a lamb," Elisabeth finished for Maria. "How about the wedding at Cana? I think that's in John." She flipped through the pages until she came to the story.

Maria rested her elbows on the table. "Well? What does it say?"

As Elisabeth skimmed this story, her shoulders drooped. "Only that Jesus turns water into wine." This was going to be harder than she had thought. But the Bible was very thick, so with a little effort, they should find something to inspire them.

Maria leaned over to study the passage more. "It says Mary was there, but it doesn't say if she drank any wine."

The friends looked at each other. "So," Elisabeth said, "if Jesus' mother drank wine, would we be allowed to?"

Maria considered it for a moment and then shook her head. "Mary was married to Joseph. Maybe that was the difference back then? We're not married, so I don't think we could. Our mothers don't drink alcohol either."

Elisabeth agreed. "What about the story about the Prodigal Son?"

"He inherited money and left, right?"

Elisabeth recalled that the father had created a grand feast for his son's return. But he did that because he had forgiven his son. "No, that's a bad idea. The Prodigal Son left to waste his inheritance."

"I'm very certain Herr Schuhmacher wouldn't do something like that."

Elisabeth's eyes opened wide. "Of course not! No, we can't use the feast that the father throws his son." Elisabeth sighed and tried to think of any other well-known feasts in the Bible.

"How about when Jesus feeds the thousands?" Maria suggested. "I know we're not feeding that many people, but we still might find an idea."

Elisabeth perked up. "Of course! Maybe there was more besides fish and bread."

Elisabeth thanked God for giving her the discipline to study so well for her confirmation before Easter. She remembered that the story of Jesus feeding thousands was also in Matthew and flipped back to it, turning the Bible on an angle to make it easier for Maria to read.

"Wait a moment." Maria pointed to the end of the story.

"It says here that Jesus fed five thousand men, without women and children."

Elisabeth had never read the Bible when trying to prepare an evening for guests, so she had never paid attention to details like this one. "Does that mean the women and children were also fed, so Jesus gave food to more than five thousand people and didn't include them when they counted everyone?"

Maria shrugged. "It could also mean that He didn't feed them."

"Why would Jesus not feed women and children?"

"You're right. That makes little sense. So it must mean that He fed everyone and they only counted the men, not the women and children."

Elisabeth sighed as she closed the Bible. "It's just as well. I'm not allowed to buy anything, I don't know how to fish, and I can't serve only bread. We have to start over." She walked through the kitchen to the back room and returned the Bible to its place on the shelf. Did everyone in their community spend this much time planning an evening? If they did, how did they get anything else done?

Elisabeth poured them both a cup of water in the kitchen and then joined Maria again in the front room.

Maria took a sip and studied her cup for a moment. "What if you kept it simple for your first evening? A few different kinds of cookies, some tea if your mother lets you buy some. Maybe doing an extra chore or two might change her mind? If not, then chamomile or peppermint would be fine."

"That's what Mammi had said—chamomile or peppermint. But won't people complain that it's too boring?"

"No, not at all! Lissika, your icing decorations...no one in Semlak can do better! I'm certain if you offer some *kipfel* dusted with icing sugar and some shortbread with your icing decorations, everyone will love it."

Elisabeth's shoulders relaxed. She could finally picture the evening unfolding, but she didn't want to bake *kipfel*.

"Tata's favourite dessert is rum cake," she said. "I'll bake a rum cake so I can practise for the welcome home celebration, but shortbread is easy so I'll have time to make beautiful decorations. Oh! And I'll draw the desserts into my sketchbook each time I host an evening. Then Tata can see how hard I worked at it."

"And how much you've missed him."

Seven months had passed since Tata's departure, and although Elisabeth had become used to his absence, she still noticed it. The biggest hole was in their household itself: every time they needed something repaired or moved, they had to find a man to help them. Georg and Stefan often did, but they had their own work and duties to tend as well. However, had Tata not left, Elisabeth would never have learned how to drive a wagon. She enjoyed the freedom very much. She would, of course, have given it up if it had brought Tata home sooner, but if she was to be honest with herself, something good had come out of Tata's absence.

"Now who to invite," Maria said, interrupting Elisabeth's thoughts. Maria jumped in her seat. "Stefan's sister! You and Stefan like each other, so it would be nice if you invited someone from his family. If it's appropriate, of course."

Elisabeth clapped her hands to her cheeks. "I feel so terrible—in all of this planning, I never once thought of her."

Maria patted her best friend on the shoulder in comfort. "It's not surprising, Lissika. She leaves immediately after church every Sunday. She may not even want to come."

CHAPTER NINE

The next evening, the Roths and Opa ate supper together. Juliana scooped mashed potatoes onto her plate and passed the serving dish to Dad. With Mom's work schedule and Dad's old driving schedule, she was used to Opa being her sole dinner companion. She had to admit that having Dad home was nice at times like these. The kitchen was crowded—there was barely enough space for the major appliances, the wall cabinet for dishes, a smaller set of cupboards that also included a shelf for the television, and a round table in the centre that seated four —but Juliana loved seeing her immediate family all at the table together.

She often enjoyed the conversation, too, so long as it didn't involve her marks (she was doing much better than when they had first arrived), old people's health problems

(Opa's favourite topic), or the latest tip Dad had learned from his courses.

But Juliana's bubble of joy popped when Dad brought up fashion.

"Katy, I really think she should be wearing longer shorts."

Mom picked up the plate of maple-glazed chicken breasts and passed them to Dad. "Or what? Boys will be after her? Seriously, Paul. This isn't the old country."

Opa chuckled at the joke. "She's right, Paul."

Dad cast Opa a sidelong glance. "Thanks for the support, Peter." He passed the chicken to Juliana, who served herself and then passed it to Opa.

Juliana knew it was now or never. She and Sophie had agreed that the parenting book could ease Dad into the topic, like how some teachers at school passed out text-books on the first day and walked you through them.

"Hold that thought, Dad." Juliana jumped up from the table, retrieved the book from her bedroom, returned, and handed it to Dad.

"What's this...?" He studied the cover and raised an eyebrow. "A parenting book?"

Mom burst into laughter. "Juliana, that's brilliant!"

"On teens," Juliana added, keeping her voice light and happy. "It promises to show you how to properly empower your teen and help her thrive in today's world by moti-vating her toward independence." She had memorized part of the text on the back. "And what parent wouldn't desire that for his child?"

Opa took the book out of Dad's hands and read the cover, turned it over, and read the back. Shaking his head, he handed it back to Dad. "Times are so different! We didn't need books to raise the three of you!"

Dad placed the book on the table and served himself some peas. "And I don't need a parenting book, thank you very much. Your shorts are still too short." He narrowed his eyes as he passed the peas to Juliana.

Mom picked up the book and studied it herself, her smile never disappearing. "Where did you get it?"

"At the bookstore in Belmont Village."

Opa shovelled a large pile of peas onto his plate, and without passing the serving dish to Mom, scooped a spoonful into his mouth. "There's a book for everything these days. Why do parents need books to tell them how to be parents?"

Dad lifted his chin and nodded at Opa. "Thank you! That's what I'd like to know."

"Irmgard and I were very good parents."

Mom snorted and almost dumped the serving spoon piled high with peas on her plate. A few peas rolled onto the table. "Tata, you wouldn't let us do anything!"

"You and Annie danced."

"Fine, but that was it. We couldn't go to any evening

parties or join after-school clubs. And what about Peter? He wasn't allowed to even dance."

"He was a boy. Boys don't dance. And look at him now! He's travelled the world, speaks English, German, French, and now he's learning Japanese from Brian. He didn't need to dance. But that doesn't matter. A father's job is to work and bring money home. A mother's job is to look after the household and children. If she wants to work, too, she can."

Juliana's eyes popped out of her head. "How is a mother supposed to accomplish all that?"

Mom chimed in. "Excellent question, sweetheart."

Opa picked up his knife and cut his chicken breast. "She doesn't have to work if it's too much. But a household needs someone at home. You're lucky I'm home to keep an eye on Juliana."

Now Juliana's mouth dropped open. She knew Opa had some old-fashioned ideas, but she assumed that since he accepted Uncle Peter's sexuality, he also accepted more equality between men and women. But Juliana didn't feel any anger toward her grandfather. More shock, if anything. No one had ever said anything like this to her face before.

Dad cleared his throat. "Well, um, I wouldn't go that far, Peter. I think it's great that Katy manages the grocery store. Besides, Juliana's old enough to take care of herself now."

Juliana clapped her hands. "Exactly! So you can stop hovering!"

Mom laughed. "You walked right into that one, Paul."

Dad raised his hands in surrender. "I guess I did." He inspected the book again. "Okay, look, I'm really busy with my college courses, but fine. I will humour you, *if I have time*, and maybe read a chapter or two. Given that your mom read umpteen books from the time she was pregnant with you until you were maybe in grade two, I guess I'll read a few chapters of one. But as I said, *if I have time*. The book won't change my mind: I still think your shorts are too short."

Juliana hoped he would read the entire book. Had she been expecting too much? Then she recalled that Dad wasn't a strong student back in his high school days. He was probably going to be a difficult student now, too. She accepted his offer and made a mental note to set up another meeting with Sophie. They needed a Plan B.

CHAPTER TEN

Elisabeth thanked Jesus that the hides hadn't been ready for her to pick up the day before. It gave Elisabeth an excuse to drive the wagon by the church where Stefan would be tending to the grounds, a job he had finally found.

But asking about his sister made Elisabeth nervous. Stefan rarely spoke of her, yet she attended church with her family every week. Not all siblings got along, but who could not get along with Stefan? He was compassionate and funny. The war still haunted him, but Elisabeth had never seen him have waking nightmares as Georg did.

Maybe it wasn't her place to ask? She could just drive by. Stefan looked very busy cleaning the stairs and pillars by the church's main entrance. Disturbing him would not be a good idea.

Then he turned around, saw her, and waved.

She needed to ask. Elisabeth's intention was to be friendly and caring, not nosy. Stefan would understand. She pulled up and tied the reins to a tree along the side of the churchyard. The yellow building with its single steeple still did not have its two bells: they had been melted down and made into cannonballs for the war, like the bells of the three other Christian churches in the village.

Even on a beautiful day like today, she thought, *I can't ignore what the war has done to us.*

Stefan wiped his hand on his pant leg and doffed his cap. "What brings you here?"

Elisabeth blushed. This reaction in his presence appeared so quickly that she could never hide it. No wonder everyone knew they liked each other. *I suppose the fact that we dance with each other at every Sunday dance might be another hint*, Elisabeth thought.

Noticing a rag in the pail, she squeezed it out and began wiping down the other pillar, despite Stefan's protestations. It calmed the flutters inside her. Besides, did Martin Luther not say that hard work was important for the soul?

"You are allowed to talk," Stefan said with a grin.

Elisabeth blushed again. She could stand up to her uncle for Georg when it was necessary, even to other people, yet to ask Stefan about his sister was so difficult. Why? She swished the rag in the soapy water, wrung it out, and continued scrubbing.

"How is your family?" She wanted to ease into her question, not blurt it out.

"They're doing all right, I suppose," Stefan replied. "My parents are becoming tired, as older folks do. But they're still able to work hard and support themselves and my sister."

Elisabeth thanked Jesus again for helping—now that Stefan had mentioned his sister, Elisabeth could offer her invitation without appearing intrusive.

"I have a question for you. I want to have a welcome home celebration for Tata, but I've never done one before. Maria said I should host a few *majen* evenings to practise."

Stefan plunged his scrubbing brush into the soapy water and attacked another spot on his pillar. "That sounds like a good idea, but it's not something I can help you with." He winked at her, and Elisabeth blushed again. *Majen* evenings were only for women and older girls. Although the men sometimes gathered in a different room in the house, that was not Elisabeth's plan for these evenings. "Too bad I can't come," Stefan said. "What's your question?"

Why was this so hard? She only wanted to ask about his sister. Was it because Elisabeth liked him? Or was it because his sister had never said hello to her before? Perhaps it was a little of both.

She just needed to ask.

"Would...would your sister want to join us?" She

glanced over her shoulder at Stefan. "I would be inviting just close friends and family."

Stefan cleared his throat. "I can ask her, but I think she'll say no." His expression changed to one of concern. "Of course, she doesn't mean to insult you! She just...can't."

That was something one said as a polite excuse to not want to come. Elisabeth thought back to the past four months since meeting Stefan, and she couldn't think of any reasons why Magdalena might ignore her.

Was it her bangs?

Elisabeth returned her attention to her cleaning. "That's all right." She had tried to say that nicely, but as soon as the words left her lips, she heard the disappointment in her voice. Wouldn't Elisabeth be someone Magdalena would want to meet? Stefan had met all of Elisabeth's siblings.

Stefan dropped his brush in the pail and pulled Elisabeth's hand down from her pillar, directing her attention to him. "It has nothing to do with you." He lowered his voice, his tone tender, not secretive. "Put your cloth down and let me explain." Stefan returned to his cleaning, but she understood why: he might not get paid if he didn't carry out his duties, and she certainly didn't want to be accused of distracting him.

"I had a brother named Georg—we called him Gyuri— who was two years older than me."

Had? Elisabeth worried where this conversation was going. "A brother? I'm sorry. I didn't know."

Stefan shook the brush in the pail, tapped off the excess water, and scrubbed over a stain in circles. "Our families were mere acquaintances at most before the war, and you were maybe twelve or thirteen when I left for the war. You don't have to apologize." A gentle smile crept onto his face. "It's too bad that you and Magdalena are so far apart in age—she's four years older than me. I think you would have been good friends." Then his smile faded. "Although she was never very talkative, Magdalena did enjoy good company. But when the family heard that Gyuri and I had both been captured, Mammi says that's when Magdalena became quieter. She still visited with friends, but she said little." Stefan sat on the stair, took a big breath, and let it out. His eyes were becoming red so Elisabeth looked at the wooden church doors. No man cried in public, if at all. Turning away might give him some dignity.

Stefan dropped the brush back into the bucket, dried his hand on his pants and wiped his eyes. "The guards at the prisoner-of-war camp treated us like animals to break us. They enjoyed tormenting us. This is nothing compared to that." He sniffed. Was he sad because of his sister or because of the memories her question had brought up?

"Stefan, I didn't mean to hurt you." She stood up. "I'll leave you alone to your work. I'm really sorry."

Stefan rose to his feet, too, and touched her wrist. "Don't go. If…" He seemed to search for words. "If this between us…continues…then I need to tell you this."

If this continues. He meant their courtship. Normally, hearing something like that would make Elisabeth's heart flutter. But not today. *The war has once again taken joy out of my life*, she thought. *I didn't even fight.* Looking up into his reddened eyes made Elisabeth feel as though she was seeing a side of him that only a wife should see, if at all. When Tata had left for America, he hadn't shed a single tear in front of his family.

Stefan resumed his cleaning and Elisabeth sat down on the stairs to the church's entrance again.

"Gyuri and I were sent to different camps. When I returned, I found out that he'd died."

Elisabeth gasped and her heart broke. Another death that affected someone she cared about. She shuddered. "I'm so sorry, Stefan."

He pressed his lips together and blinked a few times.

Elisabeth again turned away. "We truly don't have to talk about this. I just wanted to ask if she would like to come so I could get to know her."

The thick bristles on Stefan's brush scratched against the pillar. "If there's one thing I've learned from my captivity, it's that talking can help. I wish more people would do it." He cleaned for a little, saying nothing, and Elisabeth honoured his silence by wringing out the cloth and continuing on the other pillar. Sometimes the best way to show someone one cared was to not speak.

"Once my family got word about Gyuri's death, though, they still didn't know where I was. My parents kept up hope I was still alive, but I think Magdalena assumed I had also been killed. The Russians were unpredictable, especially because of their revolution. But that's when Mammi and Tata said Magdalena stopped visiting her friends and eventually stopped speaking to anyone except my parents. She carries too much sadness inside her."

Elisabeth wiped the tears that had fallen down her face. That great war had come to an end in November 1918. It was now June 1920. Why did war affect people for so long after it was over?

That shows how terrible war is, she thought.

Stefan sighed and slumped against the pillar. "When she saw me..." His voice trailed off and he lifted his stump.

"I remember first seeing you," Elisabeth said, her voice shaky. "You were also much, much thinner."

Stefan nodded. "We would sometimes sneak out at night to try and find scraps of food in the area." He swallowed. "I heard Magdalena crying when she was with the animals. It took her several days to just look at me."

Elisabeth stared at her hands. She couldn't have imagined that one simple question intended to bring happiness would unearth such a painful story.

"Eventually," Stefan continued, "she started to speak

with me, but she never regained the quiet joy I remember in her. And that includes not visiting or speaking with other people. She attends church only because my parents force her. Otherwise, I'm certain she would just stay at home."

Elisabeth's hand flew to her heart. All this sacrifice, and for what? Truth be told, she wasn't even sure why there had been a war, only that the men were needed to defend the empire because the Crown Prince had been assassinated. And what good did that do? The empire had crumbled anyway, millions had died, and those who survived all lived with pain—sometimes agony—because one man had been shot.

She wanted to talk more, but Pastor Fröhlich would be displeased if he saw Stefan talking while working, and Mammi would wonder why Elisabeth had taken so long to pick up the hides.

Also, this topic was too painful for Stefan. He had told her stories about his experiences in the war, but he had never shared something so personal with her.

"I am so sorry to ask about something this painful." Stefan held up his hand to protest, but Elisabeth spoke before he said anything. "I mean it. But I asked you about Magdalena because I truly do want to get to know her. Please ask her, just so she knows someone is thinking of her. I won't be offended if she says no."

Stefan nodded in acknowledgement. His eyes had become clear again and his smile had returned.

"I should go," Elisabeth said. "I still have to pick up hides for Mammi." She finished wiping the spot she was working on.

Stefan shook his head. "You are one remarkable young woman, Elisabeth Schuhmacher."

Elisabeth rinsed the dirt off the cloth in the bucket, squeezed it out, and laid it over the side. "She is part of your family, and I would like to get to know her better, even if she doesn't want to say much. I can also knit or crochet or embroider next to someone and not need to speak at all. It would be a welcome change from all the noise at home!"

Stefan followed Elisabeth as she returned to her horse and wagon. Although she didn't need help climbing onto the bench, he offered his arm anyway.

"You know what?" he asked. "If you practise enough, your celebration for your father might be so perfect that he'll never want to leave again." A twinkle in his eye, Stefan untied the reins from the tree, handed them to Elisabeth, and doffed his cap as her horse trotted off.

Although she understood his comment as a friendly joke, Elisabeth couldn't help but wonder if Stefan was right. If she planned a welcome home celebration that was perfect and showed Tata how much he had truly been missed and how much his family loved him, maybe he wouldn't leave again. Ever.

She needed to start hosting guests by herself imme-diately.

CHAPTER ELEVEN

Juliana stood on the porch of the Morgan household, breathing in the scent of a lilac tree that had grown beside the stairs, and holding the envelope Uncle Peter had given her with the photos, but she didn't want to go in just yet. She returned to the sidewalk and stared at the monstrous factory across the street where Opa, Uncle Peter, and maybe even Georg had worked. It took up an entire city block. On this side of the factory, she could see the original red-brick building with windows. Above that portion stood a blue...chimney? She couldn't tell. Attached to the original building but set farther back was a shorter blue addition, obviously newer than the red-brick section.

She pulled the photos out of the envelope and studied them, trying to picture where in the massive building they would have been taken. Each photo had machinery in the background, which suggested that they had been taken inside. The red-brick portion resembled the old part of Eby Heights, her high school. Only that chimney and some external piping made it look like a factory.

Her curiosity getting the better of her, Juliana crossed the street, wove around the cars in the parking lot, and found what looked like a public door in the blue section.

"I wonder if Opa walked through this very parking lot every morning," she said to herself. "And Georg, too, maybe?" The moment she thought of Elisabeth's cousin, an unfamiliar sensation arose in her. Georg had passed away sometime ago, and yet knowing he might have been here, perhaps standing exactly where she stood now, somehow brought the past to the present, even bringing her great-grandmother to Kitchener. Elisabeth had died in Romania; Juliana would never find any hint of her here. But the many drawings of Georg in her sketchbook suggested Elisabeth was close to him. It was as though Juliana could sense a family bond. Suddenly, this monstrous building that had been sitting here for who knew how long now meant some-thing to her.

Juliana continued across the parking lot and entered a door in the blue section. What greeted her was a cavernous interior with a cement floor. *It has to be two or three times bigger than the gym at school*, she thought. Along the outside walls were office doors. Was this where the managers worked?

A young woman dressed in jeans, a blouse, and heeled boots exited one office, smiled at Juliana, and asked if she could help.

"Actually, I just wanted to look. My grandfather worked here a long time ago."

"In the tire factory?"

Juliana nodded.

"I've only been in this building a couple of years, but it's not part of the rubber factory anymore." The woman blushed. "Well, sort of. It's hard to explain. But these are different businesses in here. I don't really know more than that."

Juliana wanted to ask the woman about the photos anyway. She removed the photos from the envelope again. "Do you know where these pictures might have been taken?"

The woman took the photos into her hands and examined each one. "These would definitely be in the factory itself—though I don't think they allow visitors. That's a separate company from what we do in here. I do know that this part was used to store the tires when they came off the line. Rows and rows of tires, if you can imagine that."

Juliana stared down the length of the cavernous room. Quite frankly, she couldn't imagine that. The space was far too big to imagine storing anything smaller than an airplane.

The woman shrugged. "But that's all I know. Sorry!"

"Which is more than I knew two minutes ago!" Juliana tucked the photos back into their safe spot. "Thanks so much for the help!"

The woman smiled. "No problem!"

Juliana left and returned to Aunt Anne's house before everyone wondered where she'd gone. When Aunt Anne answered the door, Juliana told her what she'd just learned.

"I thought a bit more after your birthday the other night," Aunt Anne said as she stepped back to let her niece in. "If I recall, Karl worked on the fourth floor. That's where they made the really big tires, like the ones used on tractors and trucks. Big men worked up there." She laughed. "Tata wasn't big enough, and Karl teased him about it all the time."

Juliana wondered if Georg might have worked there, too. Elisabeth had always drawn him as a big man, and Opa said the way to recognize Georg in those drawings was by his size.

Aunt Anne smiled. "You know, I remember driving by that factory at night coming home from dance or a friend's house, and the green windows on that tower spooked me like something out of Transylvania. Not that I've been there."

Juliana slid the photos out again and held up the one of

Opa, Karl, and Georg. "Do you think this might have been taken on the fourth floor?"

Aunt Anne studied the photo for a moment and then shrugged. "I honestly have no idea. Opa never worked on the big tires, so I can't imagine he would've gone up there for a picture. But I've never been inside either."

Juliana put the photos away and then slid the envelope into her backpack.

"By the way," Aunt Anne said before Juliana headed upstairs. "What are you and Sophie working on? She looks like she's about to giggle when I ask her, but she won't tell me."

Juliana appreciated her cousin's confidentiality, but retraining her father was proving harder than they had anticipated. In fact, maybe having an ally or two besides her mom would help her efforts. She explained her idea to her aunt, who loved it.

Pounding footsteps announced the arrival and immediate departure of Dean being chased by Scott, wearing a red cape.

"I'm going to get you!" Scott shouted.

"Not before I take over the world!" Dean's maniacal laugh disappeared down the basement stairs.

"I have an easier answer for you," Aunt Anne said. "Just tell your parents to have another baby. That will *definitely* keep their attention off you."

"Oh, god no! I mean, kids are great and all, but the last

thing I want is a baby in the house. The walls are made of crepe paper!"

Aunt Anne smiled. "I can't argue with you there. Anyways, Sophie's upstairs. Have fun!"

Juliana bounded up the stairs, eager to continue with Project How to Train Your Father.

In moments, Juliana and Sophie sat like officials at a conference table, ready to negotiate for world peace. Juliana updated her cousin on the state of affairs and Dad's reluctance at reviewing the provided reading material. Sophie chewed on the end of her pencil as Juliana read their ideas from the café out loud. She was pretty certain Sophie couldn't read regular-sized handwriting anymore, but she also didn't want to ask in case it embarrassed her cousin.

"Email reminders, pamphlets, create a website, sticky notes—"

Sophie jabbed her pencil in the air. "My dad uses sticky notes in his office to remind himself about things, and Mom has them all over her cookbooks."

Juliana drew a star next to the idea. "But what would I remind him about? I mean, my list of grievances is huge, but I can't write fifty sticky notes."

Sophie tapped her pencil on her thigh. "Can you print them out on your computer?"

"I'd have to tape them everywhere, and Mom's picky about tape on surfaces."

"My mom is, too. Leaves residue or—"

"Pulls off paint," Juliana finished.

Their moms, despite the fighting the girls sometimes witnessed, were strangely similar. On the one hand, it felt almost eerie that two sisters could be so alike. On the other, she felt left out: she had no one she would one day resemble in bizarre ways. Even though Rebecca and Sophie had a rocky relationship, Juliana believed deep down that someday they'd get along. Who did she have?

Now that she thought about it, joining Dad on his trips when she was younger had helped her stand out among her friends in a good way: none of them had a truck driver for a dad. He wasn't a sibling, but it still made her feel close to him. At least back then.

"I've got it!" Juliana announced. "Dad's used to sitting for long periods of time in his truck, and Uncle Peter said we should have coffee or something, spend some time together."

Sophie nodded along. "So, a presentation of some kind? Like a piece of persuasive writing? We learned about that in grade five."

Juliana slapped her knee. "We'll design a presentation that will persuade him to stop hovering."

"And with Father's Day a week away, you can do a graduation ceremony!"

Juliana snapped her fingers and pointed at Sophie. "Great minds think alike, Ms. Morgan!"

"Indeed they do, Ms. Roth!"

Juliana opened a presentation app on her laptop, and the girls began brainstorming an outline.

AN HOUR HAD PASSED, and the girls had created a presentation by combining what Sophie had learned about persuasive writing in grade school and what Juliana had learned about essay writing in high school.

"You still need a title," Sophie said. "'How to Be a Father'?"

Juliana bit her lip as she considered the idea, then shook her head. "I think that might be harsh." She thought some more. "We learned in English this semester about writing for the reader. You know: writing what they want to hear. Then they'll be more receptive to your message."

"Ah... So we need a title that will be important for your dad."

"Mhmm... How about 'How to Raise a Teen'?"

Sophie chewed on the tip of her pencil again and after deliberating for a moment, nodded. "Interesting...you're offering your dad help by telling him how to raise you, but what you're really doing is telling him how to stop hovering." Sophie clapped her hands. "Another fabulous idea, Ms. Roth."

Juliana bowed her head. "Why thank you, Ms. Morgan."

Juliana typed in the title just as both girls noticed the most enticing aroma: chocolate chip cookies.

"I'd say we've earned ourselves a treat, haven't we?" Sophie asked.

Juliana shut her laptop and grabbed the photos out of her backpack. "I want to ask your mom about these photos from Uncle Peter some more."

The girls reached the kitchen table just as Aunt Anne placed a plate in the centre.

"I could hear the two of you trampling down the stairs. I thought I'd better get these on the table quickly! But be careful. They're still a bit hot."

Aunt Anne offered iced peppermint tea and both girls eagerly nodded.

"Actually," Juliana said, "it's good they're hot. Means I won't get my hands dirty before I ask you more about these." Once Aunt Anne returned with drinks, Juliana handed her the photos. Aunt Anne wiped her hands on a dish towel before taking them. "I know they were taken inside the factory, like I said before, but that's it. But do they remind you of any stories Opa ever told you?"

Aunt Anne viewed each photo again and burst into laughter. "Oh, I have tons of memories of Tata working there. I'm sorry—it was too funny. They had a lot of sports teams in the factory—curling, hockey, baseball, but no soccer. Tata and I think some Polish worker tried to start a soccer league, but no one would join them. It just wasn't as big a thing here." She blew on a cookie and broke it open. The gooey chocolate chips dripped onto her plate and she blew on the cookie again. "Some of the guys convinced Tata to join their baseball team, because they were short one man. They told him to play outfield. But he was so poor at throwing the ball that the other outfielders would always start running in his direction so he wouldn't have to throw so far."

Juliana smiled. "I really can't picture Opa in a baseball uniform. Can you, Sophie?"

Sophie shook her head. "Nope!"

Mom added, "Modr never had to wash his uniform because he never got it dirty! The guys tried to teach him how to slide, but he refused. He said he didn't come to Canada so he could break his wrist playing a sport."

Everyone laughed again. Mom snapped her fingers as she remembered something. "Speaking of clean clothes, Modr *never* did laundry on Mondays. They cleaned something or other at the factory on Mondays, and the chimney spewed out this black stuff...I don't know what it was. But it would settle around the neighbourhood. If you had your laundry outside that day, you'd have to wash it all over again. She saved Thursdays for laundry day."

She flipped through the photos again. "I can't believe Peter had these. Have you seen these, Sophie?"

Sophie turned her face away. "Sort of."

"Why don't you get your glasses, then? They're really —"

Sophie surprised Juliana by snapping back at her mother. "No, they're not!"

Sophie's mood had done a one-eighty in a split second. *What glasses?* Then it clicked. She had told Juliana once before about her glasses: they were called bioptics and had tiny telescopic lenses on them. Sophie didn't want to wear them because they literally stuck out. Sophie apparently hated them so much that she never wore them or talked about them to Juliana. *Which is why I forgot about them.*

Aunt Anne's voice sounded tight. "Sweetheart, they help you see. Why on earth would you not want to wear them? These are great photos—"

"I said, no!"

Everyone fought with their parents. That was a fact of teen and pre-teen life. Juliana remembered when she had gotten angry at Dad for not being available to get her tap shoes when she had forgotten them on her first day of dance classes in Kitchener. She was certain it would be social suicide. Was Sophie scared about the same thing? But why? Juliana would never laugh at Sophie, no matter how she looked.

"Listen, Sophie," Juliana said, her voice soft. "You've told me about them already. I'm not going to laugh at them, if that's what you're worried about."

Sophie stormed back upstairs to her bedroom. "Yes, you will!" She slammed the door so loud Juliana jumped.

Juliana squirmed in her seat as an awkward silence followed. She tried to fill it by drinking her iced tea and blowing onto a cookie, but the air in the kitchen only got thicker. "Sorry."

Aunt Anne sat down and helped herself to Sophie's tea. "It's okay." She bit into a cookie and kept chewing. "Don't take Sophie's outbursts personally." She stared at her glass. "They're directed at me, not you."

Juliana felt like the third wheel in a conflict that wasn't about her, but there was no way of getting out of this politely. At the same time, she wanted to help her cousin if she could.

"Let me show you what Sophie's glasses look like." Aunt Anne retrieved her tablet from the kitchen desk and pulled up an image. The glasses reminded Juliana a bit of what doctors on television shows sometimes wore when performing surgery. "They magnify things for her so she can see them better. They do help—I've even read about some states in the U.S. that allow people with her condition to drive so long as they wear the right glasses. But she won't wear them in front of anyone. I don't know if she even wears them when she's alone. Granted, that doesn't happen often in this house."

Juliana understood where her cousin was coming from. She wouldn't want to wear something like that in public either. But then she glanced at the photos lying sprawled out on the table. If Juliana had had Stargardt disease, Sophie's eye condition, she wouldn't be able to see these photos that so occupied her mind right now. Sophie had, on occasion, held Elisabeth's book of drawings close to her face to see better, but from what Juliana had observed, she never did that in group settings, not even in front of the entire family.

"With summer here, she's wearing sunglasses more often than she did in the winter, even when it's overcast," Aunt Anne continued. "That's really good, but that was a fight in itself last winter. But I can't convince her to wear these. There are some girls at school who are bullying her, so I'm sure—"

"Bullying Sophie?" Juliana's anger burst out of her before she noticed it. "Why? She's the nicest kid on the block!"

Aunt Anne shrugged. "Why do any kids bully? They want to feel better about themselves. The school has a zero-tolerance policy, but as far as I'm concerned, it's useless because it's still happening. The girls have threatened to destroy her special equipment at school—she uses a computer with a magnifier so she can read books and websites in large print. They also keep telling her that they've heard blind girls get a white cane for their sixteenth birthday instead of a learner's permit. It's horrendous what comes out of their mouths."

Aunt Anne pressed the heels of her hands against her eyes while Juliana's blood reached its boiling point. "How can they be so cruel? I'd love to shove a tap shoe in their faces!"

The corners of Aunt Anne's mouth curled up a smidge. "Actually, I like that image. You could do a good number on them by swinging a pointe shoe at them. The ribbon would give you more torque." She stood up, took out a container from a cupboard, and filled it with cookies. "I shouldn't be saying that kind of stuff. Those girls have mothers, too, but when I keep hearing these stories, I really wonder what kind of mother lets her child act like that. But if I step in, the school gets in a tizzy and they insist that they'll handle it. Only they aren't." She placed the lid on the container. "For you and your family. But take the lid off once you're home so they don't get soggy from the steam. And who knows? Maybe a few cookies will relax your dad a bit."

Dad. Juliana's laptop was in Sophie's room.

As though she could read Juliana's thoughts, Sophie entered the kitchen, Juliana's packed backpack over her shoulder, her gaze to the floor. She passed everything to Juliana.

"Sorry." Sophie's voice sounded like that of a mouse. "Good luck with your presentation." She shuffled upstairs.

"Thanks for all the help!" Juliana called after her, but Sophie didn't respond.

Juliana carried the backpack and cookies to the front

door and slipped into her sandals. "Listen, Aunt Anne, I meant what I said before. If...um...if it's okay...or...um...tell Sophie she can trust me. I won't laugh, and I will never say mean things to her."

Aunt Anne hugged Juliana. "I know you won't." She pulled back and then remembered something. "The pictures! They're on the table." She returned with Juliana's photos a minute later. "I got so caught up in memory lane with them, but is that what you wanted to know?"

Juliana put the photo with Georg on top. "I'm pretty sure this is Georg, one of Omama's cousins. But I haven't seen any pictures of him older like this, so I'm not entirely sure."

Aunt Anne studied it for a minute and shook her head. "He doesn't look familiar, nor does the name ring a bell. This is the guy you asked about at Peter's, right? Sorry. I've never heard of him."

CHAPTER TWELVE

The open fields outside the village always refreshed Elisabeth, though the work to maintain them tired her out. Semlak nestled right up to the south side of the Marosch River, and the lush farmland surrounded the village on all other sides: no other village was within walking distance of Semlak's boundaries. As the end of June neared, corn stalks on the *salasch* had already grown past Elisabeth's waist, and wheat stood as tall as her knees.

Elisabeth, Georg, Samuel, and Stefan were hoeing weeds along the rows of wheat. Rosina had come out today with Elisabeth and was helping Deaf-Lissi, who was expecting a child, in the house.

Sunlight came and went as clouds drifted across the sky, a warm breeze blowing over the plains. Elisabeth wore an old skirt that reached to just above her ankles and an old blouse with long sleeves. A dark blue apron that had once belonged to her grandmother, but was too worn for special occasions, protected the front of the skirt, though the hem had already turned brown with dirt. Her leather boots reached her ankles and pinched her toes, causing her feet to ache. But Mammi wouldn't make her new ones until she had a break in her own work, and the success of Mammi's women's shoes had made sure that would not happen for a long time.

Or until Tata comes home, Elisabeth thought with a smile.

"I don't know how you manage it in the village sometimes," Samuel said to the other three. They were lined up beside each other, each person in their own row. Elisabeth had to work hard to keep up with the men but she didn't want to be stuck on her own and miss sensible adult conversation.

"How so?" asked Stefan. "I'd find it rather quiet out here." With Georg's help, Stefan had built a hoe with a longer handle for himself. This let him reach the hoe out a normal distance with his hand, then tuck the handle under the stump of his other arm as he pulled the hoe toward him. For someone who had only returned in February, he seemed to be quite practised at hoeing this way.

Unless he learned this at the Russian prisoner-of-war camp, Elisabeth realized. It was a question she would never ask him but it saddened her to think he might have been forced to labour so hard with one arm.

Samuel interrupted Elisabeth's thoughts. "At market day in the village yesterday, Herr Meier would not stop asking questions about everything and anything. People are still making comments about our agreement with Elisabeth's family. You all know me: I'm a happy, simple man. But why can't people say, 'Hello, Herr Schuhmacher. How are you?' and actually want to know how I'm doing? Instead, they asked right away about my family, and not for good reason." He paused for a moment to look at his brother. "I shouldn't bring that up, but it makes me furious."

Georg shrugged, a blank expression on his face.

Elisabeth understood what Samuel meant. The way many in their congregation treated Georg any time he was in public angered her. She couldn't even run down to Georg's house with her hair down without rumours beginning. On the other hand, though, her friends lived in the village. Although the people living out on the *salasches* often gathered together for celebrations and dancing on their own, they still lived separate from the rest of the congregation. They even had their own church service to save them the extra travel into town on Sundays. The Schuhmacher *salasch* was relatively near town at about four kilometres away, but the thirty to forty minutes needed to ride out to it meant wasted time. For those living farther away from the village—some as far as ten kilometres—it made no sense to come to town several times a week, so they only travelled on market day.

"People can be mean," Stefan replied, "but I would miss my family and friends."

Elisabeth looked at Stefan, and he smiled back at her. She was wiping the sweat off her brow when something out of the corner of her eye caught her attention. She shielded her eyes from the sun as she tried to see. A man was frantically tying his horse and wagon to a tree before dashing in the group's direction.

"Georg!" he shouted, and a few moments later, Elisabeth recognized Schubkegel Adam, who was married to Georg's sister Susi. "Georg! Samuel!"

This was not an invitation to supper. The panic in Adam's voice announced that something was wrong.

The brothers dropped their hoes. Georg sprinted to their brother-in-law, and Samuel limped as fast as he could. A childhood infection of polio had affected his ability to walk.

Elisabeth and Stefan picked up the tools and followed.

She couldn't hear what Adam was saying to Georg—Samuel still hadn't reached him yet—but watching Adam's agitation, followed by Georg's reaction, told her the situation was very serious.

"Help me unhitch my horse!" Georg shouted to Adam.

To Elisabeth's surprise, Georg's brother-in-law did exactly as he was told.

"Something is terribly wrong," Elisabeth said to Stefan, and they both picked up the pace, though Stefan passed Elisabeth with very little effort.

By the time she arrived at the front of the household, Georg's wagon had been pulled out of the way and Georg had jumped into his horse's saddle. While men in Semlak traditionally drove wagons, Georg had learned to ride on the back of a horse in the war. In a flash, Georg kicked the horse into a gallop and sped off.

"Lissika," Samuel said, turning to Elisabeth, "tell Deaf-Lissi that Tata has had a stroke. I'm going back with Adam."

"A stroke?"

"Do you need help?" Stefan asked.

Samuel looked over at his brother-in-law, who shook his head.

"Only family right now," Adam said.

"Then I'll stay here and continue with the fields."

Samuel slapped Stefan on the arm. "You are such a good friend. Thank you." He climbed up next to Adam, who snapped the reins, setting the horse into a trot.

Elisabeth rushed into the house, which was laid out the same as many of the German homes in the village. Deaf-Lissi was sitting at the kitchen table slicing radishes while Rosina stood on a short stool at the wash basin scrubbing fresh spring potatoes. Elisabeth stopped for a moment to send up a silent prayer: *Please, Lord, let him be well!*

"What?" Deaf-Lissi asked. Like Mammi, she was a woman of few words and always spoke to the point. But a moment later, her expression softened. "You're whiter than the clouds, Lissika. Is Samuel all right?"

Elisabeth raised her hands to her cheeks and felt how ice-cold they were. She nodded. "Samuel is well, but Konrad-Bátschi has had a stroke."

Deaf-Lissi's mouth dropped open. "Where is Samuel?"

"On his way with Schubkegel Adam. Georg rode ahead on his horse. Stefan is continuing in the fields."

Deaf-Lissi took a moment to survey the kitchen. Elisabeth wished she had half as much control of her emotions.

"It's best I stay here and wait for any news," Deaf-Lissi said, continuing with her vegetable preparation.

Rosina had stopped washing potatoes. "What's a stroke?"

How could Elisabeth explain a stroke? They were horrible attacks. She couldn't think of another word. Horrible attacks that came from nowhere and left the victim lame and unable to speak or otherwise help themselves. Even with the use of half the body, no farmer could contribute to the family after a stroke. They became a burden, an embarrassment. If she was honest with herself, Elisabeth believed death was more welcome than surviving a stroke, which thankfully didn't happen often.

But she had to give her sister a hopeful answer.

"A stroke is... It's like half your body is really cold and frozen and you can't use it anymore."

Rosina's eyebrows knit so tightly together Elisabeth worried they'd turn into one. "Then why can't he wear a coat?"

If the situation weren't so dire, she would have laughed at Rosina's childlike reasoning.

Deaf-Lissi stepped in. "You know how Samuel is lame? He can't walk straight?"

Rosina nodded.

"We can't make a special pair of shoes to fix it. He will always be like that. A stroke is the same, but it strikes very suddenly. Samuel was sick for a long time. But a person who has a stroke doesn't know it's coming."

"Like lightning?"

Rosina's quick understanding surprised Elisabeth. "Yes."

"Will he be better?"

Elisabeth shook her head.

"Good."

Elisabeth gasped. "Rosina! You don't say that! Lissi, I am *so* sorry for my sister's—"

But Deaf-Lissi smiled. "I think we both know what she means."

Rosina tilted her head in confusion. "What else could I

mean? Konrad-Bátschi is mean, especially to Georg, who's nice. If he's frozen, he can't be mean."

Elisabeth knew she needed to discipline Rosina for her comment, but as an uncomfortable memory surfaced in her mind, she realized she also couldn't disagree with her. Konrad-Bátschi had tried to beat Georg on the main street while Georg was fighting his own demons. Unable to make his son stop, Konrad-Bátschi had ridden off while Elisabeth remained by her cousin's side until his fit had run its course, praying Georg hadn't noticed his father abandoning him. But Georg had indeed somehow known his father had left him in the grips of nightmares from the war.

Now Stefan came in, pulling Elisabeth out of that unpleasant memory. He dried the sweat off his forehead with a handkerchief and set his hat on the table. "I wish I had Georg's strength. Keeping up with him out there has drained all of mine."

Deaf-Lissi wiped her hands on her apron. "I'll get us all a little something to eat and drink. Rosina, you can help."

Rosina nodded and obeyed Deaf-Lissi without a complaint.

Why can't she listen to me like that? Elisabeth asked Jesus. A twinge of guilt overcame her. *I'm sorry. You need to help Konrad-Bátschi and his family now. What I had to say was not important.*

Stefan thanked Deaf-Lissi and took a seat. He wiped sweat

from his face again, stuffed the handkerchief into his pants pocket, and sighed. "Georg's not ready for this. He needs time out here. Even a day's break from his nightmares is a gift from God." He turned to Elisabeth. "I'm glad your father is coming home. Georg will now have to spend all his time in the workshop. I don't know how Samuel will manage all this land."

Elisabeth froze as the consequences of her uncle's stroke sank in. In other words, if Georg didn't come out to the *salasch* anymore, her family's crop would suffer.

CHAPTER THIRTEEN

Juliana took a deep breath and dialled Sophie. She hoped her cousin would talk to her after what had happened yesterday, but she also really needed to pick Sophie's brain again: she wasn't getting through to Dad. This morning he had texted her an article he had found online about how to practise pirouettes more efficiently, at lunch he had listed—no joke—thirty reasons to not eat sugar, and after lunch he had suggested changes to her desk setup to aid in efficient studying. What would come next?

"I'm beginning to hate the word 'efficient,'" Juliana muttered as the phone rang. She crossed one leg over the other and waited.

"Hey, Juliana," Sophie answered. Her voice sounded light and happy. "What's up?"

Ignoring yesterday's events, Juliana told her cousin about what had happened. "I tried several times today to ask Dad if he'd watch my presentation, but no go. The first time he laughed at me, and by the third time he was getting impatient. But I have to listen to all his efficiency tips." Juliana tapped her foot in the air to get rid of her nervous energy.

"Hmm... That does sound like a problem."

"Your mom's cookies didn't even help. I mean, I know it's only been a couple of weeks since his new job started, but still. I'd expect to see *some* change by now."

"Does Uncle Paul like being a student at least?"

"I don't know. He probably misses the open road. When we drove here from Calgary I couldn't wait to get out of the car, but Dad was content to drive for hours. And I don't know how his college courses are going other than that he's now trying to make everything more efficient. I never asked him if he needed help because I'm scared he'll bring up some stupid health or efficiency tip."

Juliana reviewed the other ideas she and Sophie had come up with, but nothing felt like it was going to work.

"What if he's stressed?" Sophie asked. "We learned about stress management in health this week."

Juliana flipped the pencil in the air. "Actually, that could be it. Maybe Dad's stressed. Just like I couldn't wait to get out of the car, he's probably feeling the same way with not driving so much. Okay. So I need to help him relax somehow."

"Well, when my dad needs to chill, he drinks tea."

"And you and I enjoy our teas at Casimiro's. And your mom's iced tea was yummy yesterday." Juliana's hand flew to her mouth: she hadn't meant to bring up any reminders about what had happened at Aunt Anne's. "Sorry."

"It's okay." Juliana could hear regret in her cousin's voice. "I'm sorry about the way I acted. Those glasses are just...I hate them. I won't wear them and I'm tired of Mom and Rebecca trying to fix me somehow by making me wear them."

What should Juliana say? She assumed that being able to see more like everyone else did would make life easier for Sophie, but she also understood that *looking* different from everyone would not help, especially if it meant being bullied. And that was only at school. Was anything happening on social media?

The more she considered what to say, the more she realized her cousin just needed someone who understood, like she had wanted Dad to understand how embarrassing it was to not have tap shoes on her first day of class at a new studio. The situations were not entirely the same—Juliana simply wore her tap shoes at her next tap class and tried harder to fit in—but fear of rejection was similar. She had heard dancers online talk about bullying at their studios and had worked hard to find a studio whose students didn't do that. When she had researched dance studios in Kitchener, she had looked up as many dancers as possible on social media to see how they talked about one another. She chose Kitchener Dance Academy in part because most of the students appeared to be kind to each other on social media.

Sophie needs to know I'll support her no matter what, she thought.

"I don't know what it's like to lose my sight, but I know what it's like to worry about what others say about you. You can talk to me any time about things, Sophie. I promise I won't tell our parents."

There was a pause on the other end, and Juliana worried she'd said the wrong thing. Sophie could neither choose to have an eye condition nor what school to attend, and her eye disease would get worse over time, maybe requiring more assistive devices. If they even existed. She probably also worried about starting high school in two years, where she'd transition from a school with several hundred kids to one with well over a thousand. Sophie needed someone in her corner who wouldn't try to "fix" her, someone who would listen.

"Thanks," Sophie said. "But not today. Let's head to that tea shop in Belmont Village and buy your dad a bag of something."

"Awesome," Juliana said. "Meet you there in ten?"

Ten minutes later, the girls stood in front of the counter

at Claire's Tea Shop. The inside looked fairly modern, and Juliana wondered if it was one of the newer stores in the area. Since arriving before Christmas, she'd learned from her family that some of the businesses, like Casimiro's diner, had been there for decades, whereas others had opened more recently.

"Those desserts look amazing!" Juliana practically pressed her face against the display case filled with decadent desserts: filled pastries, strawberry shortcake, triple-layered chocolate cake...she was already practically drooling.

Sophie pointed to a wall of shelves behind the display case and the hundreds of jars of tea. "How are we ever going to find something for your dad?"

Her eyes wide open in amazement, Juliana only shook her head. She had no idea. She'd seen shelves of boxed teas wrapped in plastic at the supermarket, but never large jars filled with different kinds of tea. And they were all out of reach. How would she know what to ask for without seeing all the labels?

An older woman wearing a colourful summer dress with short sleeves came out of a room in the back. Her white hair flowed elegantly over her ears to just above her shoulders in soft curls. Her friendly smile rivalled Opa's.

"Hello. I'm Claire." The woman studied both girls, her expression gentle, her smile friendly. Looking at Sophie, she said, "You look like a Schuhmacher. Any relation?"

Sophie beamed. "My mom's a Schuhmacher. Anne?"

Claire clapped her hands together. "Of course! Yes, I know Anne and Phillip Morgan. They drop by once in a while. How are they doing?"

"Fine, thank you."

If Juliana ever wanted a grandmother, she'd love to adopt Claire on the spot. Maybe she and Opa...? No. A wedding ring on Claire's finger dashed that dream. *Wait a minute*, Juliana thought. *No one said grandparents had to be married to one another, right?* She could adopt Claire.

"And you would be...?"

Claire's question pulled Juliana out of her thoughts. "I'm Juliana. My mom's Katy Schuhmacher. Well, Roth now. But Schuhmacher."

Claire clapped her hands again. "Of course! But I haven't seen your mother in a very long time."

Juliana explained. "Mom moved to Calgary and married Dad. We just moved here before Christmas. We're living with Opa, um, Peter Schuhmacher." Then remembering that her grandfather and uncle shared the same name, she added, "Senior."

A look of sadness replaced Claire's smile. *Someone who wears her emotions on her sleeve, too*, Juliana thought.

"Oh, your grandmother loved to drink tea, and your grandfather would often come here after a shift at the factory to buy her something just because. Sadly, I don't think I've seen him since your grandmother passed away.

They were so much in love." Claire stood up straight and her face brightened again. "But I'm certain you didn't come here to ask about old family stories. How can I help you?"

This woman was so endearing, Juliana had to fight the urge to invite her home that day. "It's my dad. He's not really much of a tea drinker, but he's under a lot of stress."

"I see." Claire glanced at her shelves of tea. "Work related?"

"Yeah. Well, possibly. He was a trucker until a few weeks ago and now has an office job at the trucking company. But he's also taking two college courses, and Dad was never a good student. I think he misses driving."

"I see..." Claire continued, surveying her wall of teas.

Sophie added, "And now he's turned into a helicopter parent and is driving Juliana up the wall."

"The family's starting to call him Foreman Roth," Juliana said.

Claire nodded as she considered the teas lining her shelves. "There's a tea for every problem, situation, and emotion. I have just the thing, but it's in the back. Give me two minutes."

There was more tea in the back? Juliana didn't know so much tea existed in the world.

While she and Sophie waited, Juliana noticed a wall of old photos on the other side of the café and went over to look at them. As Juliana studied them, she noticed Sophie doing the same. Could she see them? Or was she just acting like she could? Some were pretty small. Should Juliana offer to describe some of them? Juliana wished her cousin could see the photos—they were beautiful and showed this tea shop was definitely not new.

But Juliana had promised herself to support her cousin, and that meant allowing Sophie to speak up when and if she wanted to. Juliana wasn't going to treat her like Rebecca—and sometimes Aunt Anne—did.

A photo caught Juliana's attention with a jolt. She grabbed Sophie's arm. "Oh my god, Sophie, look at that one!"

Sophie stepped closer to examine the photo. It was an image of the man Juliana suspected was Georg—with a beautiful, younger woman who was dressed to the nines.

"That has to be Claire and Georg."

Claire returned holding a jar. "Is everything all right? I heard someone yell." She placed the jar on the counter by a scale and some bagging supplies.

Juliana pointed to the photo. "Is that you?"

Claire squinted as she studied the photo from across the store. Once she recognized which one Juliana had asked about, she blushed. "It is. That photo was taken... oh...oh my! About fifty years ago! It was shortly after my wedding, in fact."

Juliana was too impatient to make any comments about the age of the photo. She just wanted to know if she had been right. "Is the man in the photo your husband?"

"No, no. That's George Shoemaker."

Now Sophie grabbed Juliana's arm. "Shoemaker is English for Schuhmacher, and George for Georg!"

Juliana snapped her fingers. "That's him!"

At Claire's startled expression, Juliana apologized and explained, "I'm trying to figure out some story in my family's history, and he's the key to it all. He was German, right?"

Claire cocked her head to one side. "It was so long ago... He had an accent but I don't think he was German...no, he said he was from Romania." She measured green tea leaves with other bits of...plants...into a bag.

"And his wife's name was Eva?"

Claire pointed the scoop at Juliana. "Yes, it was! Once, in the late Sixties, he went to visit his family." She returned to measuring. "He said he had been here some thirty years and only could speak to his wife at Christmas for a few minutes over the phone. Long-distance calls, especially to Europe, were very expensive back then. Other than that, it was letters and photos." Claire closed the bag and then searched across her wall of teas as she continued with her story. "He was always so sad. But, my, did he smoke. Almost as bad as the factory smokestack. He worked there for quite a while, I believe, and probably lived in Belmont somewhere, too."

She pulled a jar filled with black tea and colourful bits from a shelf. Juliana had only wanted to purchase one bag.

But Claire was so nice. Hopefully the tea wasn't expensive. Juliana only had twenty dollars with her.

"The factory actually built many of the homes in this area and sold them to the workers," Claire continued. "The managers lived in the larger homes in Westmount, behind the store here. No, wait... George was too old to have bought one of those homes." Claire shook her head. "I'm sorry. That was so long ago, I seem to have forgotten a few things. But George was so kind. I was sad when he passed away." She scooped the black tea into two smaller bags.

Someone alive who remembered Georg? Or George! Or...whatever his name was! Juliana's next question burst out of her: "When was that?"

Claire needed another moment to think back, so Juliana bounced on her toes as she waited for an answer.

"I don't remember the actual year anymore, but it was definitely the Seventies."

"The *Seventies*?!" Juliana jumped up and down at all this new information, sending Sophie into a fit of giggles.

Claire laughed. "You have about as much energy as my daughter did when she was your age."

"I've never met anyone so excited about a dead relative!" Sophie said. Juliana swatted her on the arm.

"He was a cousin. Opa won't tell me anything about him—it's a long story—and I'm trying to figure it out. You've really helped me! Can I take a photo of that photo?"

Claire approved without hesitation and closed the two

smaller bags of black tea. When the girls came to the counter, Claire pushed all three bags of tea toward the girls.

She pointed to the larger one. "This one is a green tea with peppermint, lavender, and lemongrass. It shouldn't taste too flowery for your father, but tell him to drink it while he's studying. It should help him relax and focus." She pointed to the other two.

"Oh," Juliana said. "I don't think he'll drink that much."

Claire smiled. "Not to worry. These are for the two of you, on the house. You're so interested in George, I thought I'd give you his favourite tea: a black tea blend with different flowers. George said his wife enjoyed gardening, so I told him to send her this tea so she could drink it while writing letters to him. When George read them and wrote back, he could drink the same tea as she did."

Sophie clasped her hands over her heart and sighed. "That is *sooooo* romantic."

Juliana smiled her agreement.

Claire's voice became quiet. "George was so devoted to his wife and children, and it broke my heart that he couldn't show her in person just how much he loved her. I remember how touched he was when I first gave him this tea to give her on his only visit to Romania." She took a deep breath, tucked her hair behind her ears, and pulled her shoulders back. "I never thought about any relation to your grandparents. Schuhmacher, Shoemaker—I didn't know they were the same last name. Your grandparents never said anything. You're very lucky. He loved his family like any father would, even though he couldn't be with them. It's beautiful that someone wants to remember him."

Juliana closed her eyes and drew in a deep breath. He loved his family like any father would. This did not sound like the same man Opa was angry at. She opened her eyes and touched Sophie on the shoulder. "And no one in our family remembers the true Georg."

The romanticism had disappeared from Sophie as the truth sank in and she nodded.

Claire apologized if she had upset them.

"Oh, no! Not at all," Juliana said. "It's just...um..." She didn't want to make her grandfather seem like a mean person, because he wasn't, but she didn't want to leave Claire with the impression that she'd said anything wrong. It was the complete opposite!

Sophie came to her rescue. "When Juliana arrived, she found this old book of drawing's from Opa's mother. I guess she was a cousin to Georg. George. And Juliana's been learning a lot about Opa's mom and her family, and she's been telling me about some of it, too. It's really cool. We just had no idea it was this...uh...moving, I guess."

Claire relaxed in appreciation of the explanation.

The girls paid for the stress-reducing tea and thanked Claire for everything as they headed for the door. Only after they crossed the parking lot next to the drug store to reach the path that would take them both home did Juliana speak.

"I don't get it, Sophie. Georg—or George—was here for decades. *Decades!* But no one knows him. Can Opa really dislike someone so much that he'd erase him from the family's history?"

Sophie shrugged. "He was angry with Uncle Peter a long time ago, but he's sorry about it now. Maybe this thing he has about Georg is the same?"

"I don't know. But now I'm scared to bring it up again. If Georg lived here for decades and Opa refuses to acknowledge that, then he must be super angry with him. I don't want to make Opa angry with me. You saw what happened at my birthday party at Uncle Peter's."

Sophie nodded. "Maybe it's time to drop this. We know he was here. Isn't that enough?"

"I guess..."

But in truth, it wasn't enough for Juliana. How could someone as loving as her grandfather hate another loving man? Opa had accused Georg of not being "a man," whatever that meant, and of abandoning his family. But if that was decades ago, *in the last century*, wasn't it time to move on?

But *could* Opa move on if he had that much anger inside him?

CHAPTER FOURTEEN

After putting the wagon back in its shed, Elisabeth brought the horse to its stall behind the summer kitchen and workshop. Her body ached all over: her arms were about to fall off, her thighs were burning, and her feet throbbed from wearing her tight shoes. At least Rosina had slept in the wagon. That had lifted her spirits. Once they'd arrived home, she had jumped out and gone inside. Elisabeth, however, was ready to fall asleep next to the horse in its stall despite it only being early evening. *I'll ask Mammi if there's any mending I can do*, she thought. *Then I can help while I rest.* But the moment she opened the house door and entered the kitchen, Anna announced her arrival and Mammi scowled at her.

"You unhitched that horse slower than a turtle! It's about time you joined us."

Elisabeth groaned and Mammi glared at her. Elisabeth wished she'd had a sore throat and couldn't speak.

Mammi had already put Rosina to work folding laundry. In the front room, Luki sat at the table, rag cloths over the table, covered by pairs of shoes Elisabeth didn't recognize lined up side by side.

So, he can polish other people's shoes but not his own? Elisabeth thought. *That's very unfair.*

"Rosina," Mammi said, her voice stern, "I told you that if you do not fold that laundry perfectly, you will do it again."

Rosina's mouth turned upside down—an expression all too familiar to Elisabeth—but one look from Mammi straightened Rosina's mouth out. She picked up the pillowcase she had just attempted to fold and started over.

Anna worked next to Mammi at the kitchen table, shelling peas and ripping lettuce. Several baby tomatoes sat in a bowl next to her.

"Is that supper?" Elisabeth asked.

"What do you think?" Mammi replied. Her lips pressed together and her forehead wrinkled in concentration though she was only making a salad. "Why would I be making supper for us when you can do that? This is for Margarethe's family."

So the shoes were likely for her aunt and uncle's family, too. Elisabeth swallowed her anger and made note to tiptoe around Mammi this evening. Mammi always did her duty, but with the pile of orders on her work bench, she would not be in a good mood for the rest of the night.

She needs a nap, too, Elisabeth thought. "I can take over."

Mammi snapped at her. "We won't have anything to eat if you do this. You can prepare the bread dough to rise for the night, then get sausage, pickles, and cheese from the cellar. We'll have the rest of our old bread for supper."

Why did Mammi become angry like this? It seemed like no matter what Elisabeth said or how she tried to help, Mammi was angry with her. On her way around the house to the cellar, Elisabeth silently asked Jesus what to do to help Mammi feel better, but as usual, He said nothing. Wouldn't it help to return the favour and talk to those who talked to Him?

Back in the kitchen, her apron full of food plus a ball of sourdough from the previous bake and some fresh yeast, Elisabeth set everything on a table in the corner, out of Mammi and Anna's way. Then she pulled out the bread trough from under the wall unit where they stored the dishes and cutlery. Carved out of a tree trunk, it allowed the family to prepare and bake a week's worth of bread instead of just one loaf at a time. Mammi automatically cleared half the kitchen table for the trough. The bag of flour was already on a chair. Elisabeth washed her hands in the ceramic wash basin, dried them well, and began scooping flour into the trough.

Elisabeth wondered what Mammi had seen at her

brother-in-law's house. If someone didn't die after a stroke, they were often kept in a room by themselves, with only the closest family and friends allowed to visit. Elisabeth remembered maybe once or twice seeing someone after a stroke. She could feel their humiliation. Despite how horribly Konrad-Bátschi treated his oldest son, Elisabeth would not wish such a condition upon anyone.

And what if he died? When a husband died, his widow usually remarried because a woman needed a man's help to support her family. But with fifty fewer men in the village because of the war, and too many young men not yet finished with their military service, that left few options. Elisabeth did not like her aunt either, but she was grateful that Margarethe-Néni would not need to remarry: her children were all grown and married themselves, and with two sons, she would always have somewhere to live. *Although I don't know if she would enjoy life on the* salasch, Elisabeth thought.

"Give me that." Mammi grabbed a knife out of Anna's hand before Anna started chopping a head of lettuce and used it to cut up some green beans.

Anna's startled face caused Elisabeth to switch places with her, and Mammi didn't object. Anna dried her hands and continued scooping flour from the flour bag into the bread trough. Elisabeth got herself a knife so she wouldn't have to share with Mammi.

The knife in Mammi's hand flew as she chopped. "I

cannot believe we let Georg help us as we do. If it were not for his fits, his father would still be standing." She whipped the cut green beans into a bowl, threw the next batch of beans onto her cutting board, and continued.

Elisabeth's fingers tightened around the handle of her knife, its blade hitting the wooden board harder than usual as she chopped the head of lettuce. She had to stand up for her cousin: war, nightmares likely for the rest of his life, and now his father on his deathbed. How could anyone shoulder such a burden? What if Mammi had spoken her thoughts to Georg? He already carried the guilt of losing her brother with him. If Mammi blamed him for his father's stroke, Elisabeth was certain he would believe her.

But Elisabeth feared Mammi would yell at her if she said anything. What point was speaking up for someone if you were going to get in trouble, too? This wasn't her uncle or other members of their community: this was her mother. She could punish Elisabeth, make her do more chores, and make her life more difficult.

Mammi whipped the chopped beans into a bowl and threw the next handful of whole beans onto her board. Her lips stayed pressed together, her face still wrinkled in concentration.

Mammi became angry if people didn't do their duty or if they stuck their nose in her business where it didn't belong. But she also became angry when she was sad. Tata would talk to her alone, and Elisabeth had tried that before, too, with some success. But she still felt compelled to say something now, despite her siblings being present. Accusing Georg of almost killing his father was too serious an accusation to leave on the table.

Perhaps she could give Mammi a gentle reminder of how things had changed in the last couple of months?

"Without Georg and his brother, we wouldn't have corn and wheat growing, and Anna would have had to stay home while her ankle healed. In fact, Anna wouldn't have even been found by anyone for quite some time after those boys pushed her and she sprained her ankle."

Mammi pointed the knife at Elisabeth. "Georg set Anna on top of that horse. How shameful that was!"

Elisabeth tried hard not to roll her eyes. Anna had been sitting sideways—her legs were not on either side of the horse—and Georg had had no other option except to carry her the entire way home. Even with his strength that would have been impossible.

"If he had made her walk, she would have hurt her ankle even more. He does his best to help us where he can. You thanked him for his help just a couple of months ago."

Mammi glared at Elisabeth and then returned to chopping beans. "That was before his father's stroke. I've changed my mind."

Elisabeth now pushed the chopped lettuce into a salad bowl and slammed the bowl on the table. "Those fits are not Georg's fault!" Elisabeth could glare back at her mother just as harshly.

Mammi slapped her hand on the table. "Pastor Fröhlich has said so before: Georg's fits are his punishment from God! Do you believe you know more than our pastor?"

Elisabeth dropped her gaze and stared at the wooden cutting board, the straight grooves the knife gouged out mirroring the sharpness of her anger. She lowered her voice. "Of course not."

"I should hope not. He has gone to school and is a learned man."

I read Tata's encyclopedias and listen to the news each week, Elisabeth thought. *I may no longer go to school, but I still learn.*

But Elisabeth said nothing. She prayed to Jesus to help her show Mammi that Georg was at fault neither for his fits nor his father's stroke. That was all she could do to help him right now.

Only Elisabeth's right hand moved now. Even her right shoulder complained as she lifted the pencil over a fresh page in her sketchbook. She set the pencil down and leaned back in her chair in the back room, three lanterns lighting up her sketchbook while the rest of the family slept in the front room. Sleep was far from the angry storm of her mind. A stroke seemed to leave the victim's soul caught between earth and heaven. Some families even hid away their lame, mumbling sick members to avoid further embarrassment in the community.

Elisabeth recalled the short conversation she and Stefan had had at Deaf-Lissi's: with Konrad-Bátschi's condition came more expectations for his oldest son. That meant no time away at the *salasch*. What would follow, however, frightened Elisabeth the most: more fits and nightmares, more derision in the community, more embarrassment for his whole family, and even higher expectations for himself.

It was a devil's circle.

And when he and Eva have their baby? Elisabeth stared at the crucifix hanging above the doorway, her eyes pleading. *Please perform a miracle! The Bible says You cured the lame. Why can You not cure my uncle? He's now lame. Or why can You not cure my cousin? He is a good man and can help so many people, but with his fits he is pulled into a world of death and sadness against his will. I know it's not Your fault that these things have happened, but just like it's not my fault if someone's house goes on fire, I still help them get away from the flames.*

Georg would now need to dedicate all his spare time to his and Konrad-Bátschi's blacksmithing work, leaving the field work on the Schuhmacher *salasch* to Samuel, Deaf-Lissi, and Elisabeth, with occasional help from Stefan. She did not shy away from physical work, but she could not deny that she was weaker than the men because she was a young woman and was therefore unable to work as fast as they did.

You have all the power in the world and You're allowing my uncle to suffer like this.

Suffer. Her uncle was now suffering. Did he think about Georg? About the suffering he caused his own son? About the suffering Georg lived through every day?

"And what about Tata?" she whispered to herself. "I'm certain he can't wait to see his brother again. What if his brother dies before he returns home?"

Or was God punishing her father for leaving his home in search of riches? Tata had not taken his inheritance like the Prodigal Son had, but he had left his home.

"No," she said to herself. "I'm going in circles now. God punishes bad behaviour and lazy workers. Tata left so he could earn more money and give us a better life. Several families in Semlak have relatives in America who send money back. These families have shingle roofs instead of straw ones like we do. I've even heard through Maria that they have a new kind of oven, one that keeps a jug of warm water inside it." Depending on Mammi's mood, Elisabeth didn't always have time to warm up water to wash up with. It was much more pleasant to wash her hair and face in warm water.

But none of these thoughts put out the fire burning inside her and soon she gave in to it, aching shoulder and all. Her pencil pinched between her fingers glided a dark, thick lines across the page.

"Now I can't even have my evening of *majen*." The idea raised feelings of guilt in Elisabeth—how could she think about having friends over when her uncle was sick? But she had placed high hopes on these social evenings to prepare to please Tata with a beautiful celebration for his homecoming. With the entire Schuhmacher family now busy with Konrad-Bátschi's care, Mammi would not allow Elisabeth to hold any kind of social evening.

She paused as she again looked up to Jesus hanging on His cross. "I know I shouldn't feel this way. Of course Konrad-Bátschi is more important than a social evening. But having that evening meant so much to me!"

Her fingers dashed again around the page and an overturned table appeared, its harsh, heavy lines reflecting just how deeply her anger pushed into her soul. Tata wanted her to draw all the important events that happened to her while he was gone, and being angry at God was certainly one of them, but since she didn't know what God looked like, she had to show her anger in a different way.

Elisabeth lost all sense of place as she drew and shaded, adding two overturned chairs to her drawing, followed by broken dishes. She didn't know how much time had passed by the time she finished.

She raised her eyes to the ceiling. "God? Do You see this?

This is what Tata is coming home to. Do You understand? This is Mammi's chair, and this is Georg's chair. Two months ago, Mammi thanked Georg for all his help, and now she despises him again. Why? Tata wanted us to get along with his family. He told me in a letter a long time ago. Now Mammi despises Georg again. What will Tata say when he sees all this fighting?"

Realizing she was speaking aloud and that her voice was raised and might wake her family, Elisabeth flipped the page over and let the anger explode through her fingers instead, her pencil scratching ferociously at the paper. But this time, her anger refused to travel in straight lines. It sought curves, and as an image formed in Elisabeth's mind, her heart raced. She saw Georg's horse speeding off, unhindered by a wagon, and heard the hooves of Georg's horse beating the ground as he raced to the village, the pounding becoming quieter as he disappeared down the road.

She studied her drawing—the hooves of his horse in a gallop, Georg's foot in one of those loops that hung down from the saddle—and felt it couldn't quite express that hammering sound that mirrored both her anger at God for not helping and the fear that Georg's life was about to change for the worse.

CHAPTER FIFTEEN

Juliana couldn't drop it. Why did Opa shut down every time she brought up Georg's name?

"I can at least ask him to tell me how he and Oma came here, right?" she asked herself as she walked up the driveway. "Maybe he'll say something as he's talking? And if he doesn't, at least I won't make him angry." Opa loved talking about his past and his family—he just didn't like Georg.

When she entered the house, Opa was slicing summer sausage and setting the slices on a plate with some crusty white bread, butter, and cheese.

"Hello, Yulika," he said.

"Hi, Opa. That looks good."

Opa patted his stomach. "I'm eating a little before Karl picks me up. Otherwise I'll eat like a pig there and embarrass myself in front of all our friends!" He laughed. "Plus, it's hard to concentrate on cards when you're eating." He pointed to his head. "*Dachschaden.*" At Juliana's confused look, he translated. "Roof damage." Juliana laughed. There were some days when Opa was sad about his declining memories. Other days, he joked about it.

Juliana got herself a glass of water. "So, you're going to play cards?"

Opa nodded. "Fred Perkins is visiting. He used to work at the factory with us. Karl called a few other friends from the old days so we can all play cards together."

"That sounds like fun!"

Opa smiled. "It will be!" He sat down at the table and pushed his plate toward Juliana. "Fred was a bead coiler."

Juliana scrunched her face in concentration as she tried to imagine what a bead coiler was. Her mind came up blank.

Opa separated a slice of his sausage from the others. "Do you see this?" Opa traced a circle around the edge of the sausage, and Juliana nodded. "Pretend this is a tire." He scored another circle a few millimetres in. "This is where the rim and wall meet. The beading goes in here. It's steel wire coated in rubber. That's what a bead coiler made."

Juliana picked up a slice of the summer sausage and studied it for a moment before popping it in her mouth. "But I bet you couldn't eat it!"

Opa smiled sadly. Juliana had expected a bigger reaction from him. Was it his Alzheimer's?

"No," Opa said, "but we breathed it in. The chemicals, I mean. Whenever I had to blow my nose, black stuff would come out."

"Black stuff? Like, it would be in your tissue?"

Opa nodded. "From the carbon black. That causes cancer." He pulled his plate back and began eating.

Juliana tried hard to keep swallowing her sausage. That was why Opa had suddenly become sad. This wasn't the direction she wanted the conversation to take. She had to turn it around fast.

"Opa, how did you meet Karl?"

He bit off a piece of his bread and talked, despite his mouth being full. "We grew up in Semlak together."

Juliana slapped her hand on the table in excitement. "Does that mean he knew your mother?"

Opa nodded. "His mother and Mammi became good friends. Everyone made fun of her because she had a crooked nose. But Mammi didn't like that and thought she was nice."

Juliana decided that now was a good time to make some tea if she was going to get Opa to talk more. She pulled the bag of tea that Claire had given her out of the shopping bag. She checked the instructions and asked Opa if he knew how to make loose-leaf tea.

Opa inspected the packaging. "Oh! It's from Claire?"

Juliana nodded. "I haven't seen her in a long time."

"She says hi. She was very friendly."

Opa pointed at Juliana. "Sometimes she made friends too easily."

"What do you mean?"

Opa waved his comment away. "Nothing. You want to make black tea? Do you like it?"

Juliana shrugged. "I've never tried this kind before. It smells nice."

He opened the bag and held it to his nose. "I know this smell." Opa stuffed a slice of summer sausage in his mouth and walked into the living room. He rummaged through a cupboard in the wall unit and brought out a mesh ball. "Your *oma* used this to make tea for herself sometimes."

He handed it to Juliana, and she inspected it. The mesh ball had a short chain attached to one side, and a clasp held both halves of the ball closed. The instructions on the label said to boil the water, so Juliana filled a mug with tap water and placed it in the microwave. While the water was heating up, she used a small spoon from the cutlery drawer to measure a teaspoon of the tea into the mesh ball. The microwave beeped, and Juliana used a tea towel to lift the hot mug out and place it on the table. She pulled out her phone, set the timer to three minutes as the instructions had said, and dropped the mesh ball with the tea into the water.

As the tea steeped, though, Opa stared at it and kept taking deep breaths. "I know that tea." His face darkened, as though he was remembering something, but he kept repeating that he recognized the scent wafting from the cup. Juliana wondered if she should dump the tea—it was upsetting him, and she suspected she knew why.

Trying to draw his attention away from the mug, she asked, "So did you and Karl come to Canada together?"

His gaze still fixed on the mug, Opa replied, "No. Karl came first. We came two years later."

"And he got you the job at the rubber factory?"

Opa's eyes opened wide in sudden recognition. "This is Georg's tea, isn't it?"

Juliana stared at the mug now, too, not wanting to see Opa's anger. "Claire gave a package to both me and Sophie. He drank it when—"

Without finishing his food, Opa left for his bedroom in the basement. "When he wrote letters to the wife and children he left behind. That tea stinks."

A minute later, Juliana heard the door to Opa's bedroom close.

She sighed as she remembered that smell was powerful at reawakening memories. It had never occurred to her, especially because she didn't expect Opa to recognize the scent.

Her phone alarm rang, and she lifted the mesh ball out of the cup, though she had no desire to drink the tea now.

Part of her felt guilty for upsetting her grandfather yet again, but the part of her that was drawn to this puzzle about Georg had cause for celebration: Opa had just confirmed her suspicions. He had indeed met Georg here in Kitchener.

That left one question unanswered: Yes, the man left his family behind, but if he had died over forty years ago, why couldn't Opa forgive him?

CRAMP ROLL, cramp roll, cramp roll, cramp roll.

A and a one, a and a two, a and a three, a and a four.

The sounds Juliana created through her feet echoed those of a galloping horse, with each step making four sounds to one beat in the music. Mom had taken Opa to church that morning, so Juliana tapped without worrying he would watch. This left her emotions free rein to flow through her as she tried to sort out her dilemma: how could she solve this puzzle without further upsetting her grandfather? As she often did when she was upset, she had sought guidance in Elisabeth's drawings. The emotion in the sketch of the horse's legs and a man's foot in a stirrup reflected the emotions this entire situation had caused within her: anger at a family secret, urgency to solve it, longing to help deal with the outcome, whatever it would be.

Pull back, pull back, pull back, pull back.

A and a one, a and a two, a and a three, a and a four.

Even the names of some of the steps reflected Juliana's journey into this challenge that went beyond words: *tapping* Opa's stories for dropped clues, *shuffling* her emotions around as each piece of information came to light, *pulling back* from asking Opa as perhaps she should have done on Wednesday.

She continued mimicking the gallop of a horse while she stared at the drawing, the book open on a shelf against the wall. Who was on that horse, and where was he going so quickly?

The beat of music pulsed through Juliana as she allowed her feet to drum out the rhythms on her tap board in Opa's basement.

She wanted to discover the full story about Georg. No more secrets. It was clear Opa—for whatever reason— wasn't sharing something with the family. Something important.

Heel flam, heel stomp. Heel flam, heel stomp.

And one, and two, and three, and four.

Juliana raised her gaze toward the ceiling. "But what? What isn't he telling us?"

She continued tapping, now switching up her rhythms. If she could just get Opa to understand how traumatized Georg must have been, to *really* understand that, would he change his opinion? Would he open up? All Opa ever said about this cousin was that he had deserted his family because he couldn't control his fits, and that he could only work for a few hours a day in his blacksmithing shop before succumbing to "shakes." Did Georg suffer from post-traumatic stress disorder? Did he come to Canada to stop any hallucinations and panic attacks his PTSD caused?

But if that was the case, then why hadn't Georg's family immigrated to Canada, too? Why wasn't there a slew of distant cousins for Juliana to meet?

A new song came on, this one with a faster, stronger beat, and Juliana's feet changed their rhythms to match. She bent her knees deeper to sink her weight closer to the ground so she could express every sound. She felt as though she was squeezing every drop of energy down to the soles of her feet. The drumming in the song built up, and Juliana's feet returned to the fast rhythm of a horse speeding off, its rider urging it faster and faster. She wiped her arm across her forehead, almost tempted to drink the sweat: her mouth and throat were parched. She had pulled on her tap shoes to give her something to do while she thought, not realizing just how much emotion she had stored inside her.

If she pressed Opa further in this matter, his symptoms might worsen, and Juliana couldn't live with herself if that happened. But he was her grandfather! Why would he lie to her? To his family? Wasn't family important to him? That's what he always said. Was Opa no different from other adults who told kids to behave one way while they did the exact opposite?

Her feet pounded into the tap board. The music didn't matter anymore.

But when she turned halfway around, Juliana almost stumbled to the ground: Dad was standing in the doorway.

Why couldn't she find solace in an art form that was quiet? One that didn't announce to the entire household that something was wrong?

Juliana rushed to turn down the volume. So much for being alone. But the kind smile on Dad's face erased Juliana's momentary frustrations.

"I'd forgotten what it's like to watch you dance up close," he said. "You've come so far since we moved here. But I can't help but notice that you're angry. Is it because of me?"

Juliana bent her head forward to meet her hands as she wiped her forehead again, buying herself a few seconds to decide how to answer. She had never wanted Dad to feel guilty about what she was trying to teach him. Yes, he needed to back off, but if she let him believe that the anger he had just witnessed was because of him, that wouldn't be true. There was a time to lie to parents, and there was a time to come clean.

But to come clean meant suggesting that Opa had been lying all these years. If there was one thing Juliana had learned, though, since moving here, it was that secrets rarely kept to themselves. Even when she and Sophie had tried to look for a funny photo of Mom without telling anyone, she had landed in trouble. Then there were the lies about her marks at school, too. The photo fiasco had ended in happiness. The talks about her marks, not so much.

"Well?"

She had to tell him. One reason Juliana hated her father's previous career was because he was never around when she needed him, and right now, she needed him.

She bowed her head, scared to make eye contact. "I think I've stumbled upon a family secret."

"What kind of secret?"

"The kind of secret that could really upset Opa if I ask him about it again."

Dad said nothing for a moment, and Juliana wished she could tell what he was thinking. Another negative about his last job was that, in all honesty, she didn't know her father all that well. Once school and dance kept her busy, she would often only see him for seven or eight days in an entire month.

"Let's go upstairs, Jules. You need a drink of water and a change of clothes." His smile was gentle and disarming. Juliana whipped off her shoes, slid her tap board back under the couch, and raced upstairs to change and wash up.

Sitting at the kitchen table ten minutes later, all signs of sweat erased, Juliana gulped down a glass of water while

Dad handed her a banana, a bag of cashews, and a small plate.

"You like these kinds of snacks after dance, right?"

Juliana nodded. After getting a little food into her, she recounted everything she had learned so far about Georg and his appearance here in Kitchener. Different expressions flashed across Dad's face as she spoke: concern, anger, compassion. But by the time she was done, Dad had crossed his arms, lifted his shoulders, and tightened his lips into a firm line.

"We don't have to talk about this," Juliana said. "I'm really tired of upsetting people."

She stood up to leave, but Dad asked her in a gentle voice to sit down.

He ran his fingers through his hair and sighed. "It's not you, Jules. Not by a long shot." He took another breath and straightened out the tablecloth on his side of the round table. Juliana didn't often see Dad this agitated. She kept putting food into her mouth to make sure nothing escaped her lips as he spoke. "I've told you before that my options coming out of school were truck-driving or the military."

Juliana nodded.

"What I didn't tell you, though, was that the real reason I didn't go into the military was because my dad had died from PTSD."

Juliana's eyes went wide. Dad never talked about his

family. All she knew was that his parents had passed away before she was born.

"I don't say a lot about it because it hurts too much. I donate to the Poppy Fund every year in the hopes that other veterans can get better help, but that doesn't make things any better for me."

A million questions ran through Juliana's head: Why did his father have PTSD? What had happened to him? What had happened to Dad's mom? The questions were screaming to get out, but she didn't want to hurt her father so she shoved a handful of cashews into her mouth.

"I'll be honest with you, Jules. As much as it hurts me to hear—from anyone, not just your grandfather—that symptoms of PTSD are under the sufferer's control and can just be turned off, maybe it might be best for Peter if you don't ask any more questions."

Juliana's gut feeling had said the same thing.

"Although you may never find out why he hasn't told your mom and her siblings the whole story, you can safely assume that this Georg came here, that he and your grandfather knew each other, that he worked at the factory, and that he's buried here, if the lady at the tea shop is right. Trying to change Opa's mind now, at his age and in his condition, is probably going to cause him more distress."

She sagged against the back of her chair. "I guess I was hoping that if he had changed his opinions about Uncle Peter, he might have changed his opinions about Georg."

A kind smile appeared on Dad's face. "You've become hopeful again these past few months, like you were in Calgary. It's nice to see. You have to remember, Jules, that your uncle is Opa's son. That's different than a cousin of some kind."

Juliana sighed. "I guess."

"If you want to ask at the tea shop again, go right ahead. But I wouldn't bring it up to your grandfather again."

Juliana nodded. Dad was right. She'd have to live with this mystery.

Or find another way to solve it.

CHAPTER SIXTEEN

Mammi scrubbed the breakfast dishes in the ceramic wash basin as though she were removing a grape stain from a white dress. "That Georg could draw attention to himself like that. It was horrible! God should punish him for such behaviour." She almost whipped the plate at Elisabeth who was drying the dishes. "I counted three of his fits from the moment I arrived yesterday! As though his family has nothing more important to worry about right now."

Three? Elisabeth tried to hold back tears. From what Eva had told her in the past, Georg might have one a day, sometimes even skipping a few days before the next one. Stefan had said just as much a few days ago. Three in one day... She shuddered to think what kinds of nightmares he was having. Elisabeth was glad Rosina was feeding the animals: to hear this news would greatly upset her.

Holding a drying towel in each hand, Elisabeth rubbed the water off the plate as fast as possible to keep up with Mammi. "They're not his fault." Though she might as well have been talking to a cat. Why would Mammi start believing her today?

"Pastor Fröhlich has said that the fits are punishment for his behaviour." Mammi repeated the pastor's opinion as though she had read it straight out of the Bible. The next plate almost flew out of her hand at Elisabeth.

"But, Mammi, that doesn't make any—"

Mammi interrupted. "There is no excuse. If he would ask the good Lord for forgiveness, this would all end. I can't stand the look of him. I will say it again: I wish we hadn't allowed him to help our family. He is not a man."

This conversation had become the same as the one yesterday evening. Elisabeth said nothing more. She would need to find a way to convince Mammi otherwise. She had done it before, she could do it again. Elisabeth just needed some time to think up of ideas.

"That is why you will visit them today," Mammi said.

"Me? But I was going to help on the *salasch* again. There's so much to do."

"It can wait one day. Rosina will go with you. I cannot look after her today: I've already lost too much time. My customers will only wait so long."

Elisabeth had to take her youngest sister along? "Would Rosina not be better off at a friend's house today? Is Konrad-Bátschi's house the proper place for a child her age?" Elisabeth trapped another plate between her hands.

Mammi scrubbed and rinsed the last plate. "A child is never too young to learn how to help others."

No sooner had Mammi finished speaking than she dumped the dirty water into the slop pail. "Take that to the pigs before you go." She disappeared out the door.

Rosina came back inside. "I fed the cow and the pigs!"

"And the horse and fowl?"

Rosina shook her head. "I forgot. You should have reminded me."

Elisabeth tried not to roll her eyes. How could her sister forget all those noisy birds, with their honking, clucking, and quacking? Rosina had a good heart—all her siblings did—but she had learned how to blame others for her own mistakes.

As they walked to their aunt and uncle's house, Elisabeth reminded Rosina how to act.

"Ask how you can help. Do not ask about Konrad-Bátschi. Do *not* try to see him. But if someone looks sad or is crying, you may give the person a hug. Do you understand?"

To Elisabeth's surprise, Rosina's face was serious as she nodded. "I'll be a good girl. Jesus will be proud of me."

Elisabeth rubbed Rosina's back in approval.

When they arrived, smoke was coming out of the black-smithing workshop's brick chimney, suggesting Georg was working. Elisabeth would have offered to help him, but she didn't know the first thing about his family's trade. Besides, it was a man's job and required even more strength than farming.

Eve, Gretche, Susi, and several women from Margarethe-Néni's family were walking between the summer kitchen in the back and the house door, always carrying something: a cup of tea, food, laundry from the clothesline. After Elisabeth and Rosina passed through the front garden and the poultry yard, they came upon the summer kitchen. It was larger than the one at Elisabeth's home because no workshop had been built into it. There were wooden benches and tables to seat at least ten people. Elisabeth's stomach rumbled at the smell of mulberry jam that Eva was stirring over the stove.

Eva smiled at the sight of the two sisters, but before she could even welcome them, Rosina asked, "How can I help?"

Eva patted the top of Rosina's head and thanked her for coming. But when she embraced Elisabeth, her arms pulled Elisabeth close to her, and Elisabeth tried to be mindful of her cousin's growing belly.

"We're here to help," Elisabeth said. "I'm sure Jesus is watching and doing His best to help, too." Though, in her heart, she had some doubts. Why would Jesus allow this to happen?

Eva nodded as she let go and wiped her eyes. "Thank you." She returned to stirring the jam. "Can you look in on the pigs and make sure they have enough water? I think it's going to be very hot today. And then maybe feed the fowl?"

"I'm very good at feeding birds!" Rosina said, a big smile on her face. "I did it this morning. I'll show Lissika what to do."

Elisabeth and Eva smiled at her eagerness.

"We'll come back here when we're done," Elisabeth said. "I must be home when Luki and Anna come home so I can help them with their homework, but I can come back this evening if you need us."

Eva squeezed Elisabeth's hands. "Thank you."

Elisabeth and Rosina headed to the stalls across the yard.

"That was very kind of you," Elisabeth said.

"Jesus is watching. I want Him to know I'm a good girl." As they passed the workshop, Rosina asked if they could say hello to Georg, and Elisabeth said yes. She marvelled at the thought that just a few months before, Rosina would have run past the workshop as fast as possible to avoid seeing him. All Elisabeth's siblings had been that frightened of Georg, sometimes even cowering together on the settee in the front room to protect themselves from whatever harm they imagined he would bring to them. But as they had begun to understand him better, they lost their fear of him. *Tata would be proud of all of them*, she thought. Tata had written previously that he hoped his family would rely on his brother's family for help.

"There's a fire inside," Elisabeth warned her sister. "You must stay away from it: it's very hot. And if Georg is working, you must wait for him to come to you. Do *not* run to him, because he may be holding *very* hot metal. Do you understand?"

Rosina nodded, but Elisabeth held her hand just in case. When they arrived, though, the coals were only glowing and there was no sign of Georg.

"Perhaps he's taking a break," Elisabeth said. "Or he has gone to the store to pick up some supplies. Let's feed the animals and then maybe we'll see him afterwards."

Secretly, Elisabeth was worried. Georg was not irresponsible: he would not leave glowing coals in the workshop, and the smoke had been floating out the chimney when they had arrived. *Should I douse the fire?* she wondered. *But what if he does just leave the fire for a few moments to get something?*

She left the fire for now, deciding she would check back after they'd finished feeding the pigs.

When they entered the pig stalls, though, Elisabeth gasped and her hands shook. Georg was lying face down in the dirt. She rushed to his side while demanding Rosina say nothing: Eva already had too many worries, and after hearing Mammi this morning, Elisabeth knew that the last thing Georg needed was the family knowing something had happened to him again.

She shook him and called his name, careful not to shout. The pigs' snorting and squealing helped cover her voice.

"Is he dead?" Rosina's voice quavered as though she was fighting back tears.

Georg groaned and rolled onto his back.

"Go feed the poultry," Elisabeth instructed her sister. "He was just sleeping. I'll help him wake up."

"Sleeping in dirt?"

Elisabeth had no time for her sister's questions, as innocent as they were. "Just do as I tell you and say nothing to Eva. If she asks where I am, tell her I've carried some water to the pigs."

Rosina nodded and left the stalls, looking over her shoulder at Elisabeth and their cousin.

Georg opened his eyes.

"What happened?" Elisabeth whispered. She wanted to help clean off his clothing, but there was barely a spot *not* covered in dirt. He pushed himself to a sitting position and cursed himself as he stared at his clothes. She offered him a handkerchief to wipe the dirt from his face.

"I can't be seen like this," he said, his cheeks burning

with humiliation as he wiped them off. He handed back her handkerchief, his eyes on the ground.

Elisabeth folded it to keep the dirt on the inside and slid it back into her skirt pocket. "I can get you fresh clothes."

Georg shook his head. "You don't know where everything is. It will draw attention." He cursed again.

Elisabeth repeated her question. "What happened, Georg?"

Georg pulled a cigarette and match from his vest pocket and lit up. After a few puffs, he answered, but kept his gaze on the ground. "Ever since Tata's stroke, when these nightmares come, I see only the worst thing that happened to me. I've seen it four or five times since yesterday." He buried his face in his hands, his cigarette poking out from between his fingers.

"May I ask what it is?"

He lifted his head and studied Elisabeth for a moment, as if debating whether or not to tell her. He placed his cigarette in his mouth and took a deep breath. "There's nothing you can do about it."

"Stefan says that sometimes talking about things can help."

Georg tapped his cigarette, and ashes fell from its end. He rubbed them out under his boot. "Does he now? His nightmares aren't as harsh as mine, and I'm not surrounded by former soldiers who understand what I went through."

Was Elisabeth imagining things or was Georg upset with her for what she had said? "I'm sorry, I didn't mean to anger you."

He waved her apology away, an expression of regret on his face.

"I know I'm not a former soldier, but I'm still somebody who cares," Elisabeth said. "You can talk to me."

A gentle smile formed on Georg's lips. "You are also young and naïve, Lissika. You know and accept that the war was horrible. To know any more would trouble you."

Elisabeth's stomach began to form knots as she remembered how Konrad-Bátschi would belittle his son in public while Georg was having these fits and nightmares. It was moments like this one, right now, that proved to Elisabeth without a doubt that Georg had no control over them and that God did not cause them. What man would want to be found face down in a pigpen after reliving a nightmare? And what kind of God would do this to a man who tried so hard to change and be helpful?

"I hear the whispers, Lissika. People are blaming me for my father's condition."

"I don't blame you."

Georg stood up and removed his jacket. "You're only one person."

"Eva doesn't blame you either."

Georg sighed. "Perhaps not, but I know she doesn't believe I'll make a good father."

"Please don't say that! That's not true! The way you care for my family, Georg... You have become like a father to us."

Georg shrugged, which hurt Elisabeth. How could he not see how much he helped her family? From tending to their farmland to making sure Anna and Luki arrived at school safely and were picked up while Anna's ankle healed, Georg had given her the strength to carry on while Mammi was pregnant. When Mammi lost the baby, that was almost more difficult to deal with than Tata's leaving. How could he shrug her words off so easily?

Georg took another puff on his cigarette. "I envy your father." At Elisabeth's surprised expression, he added, "I know you miss him. But to be away from the gossip... One day, I want to travel to a country where no one knows me, one where this war was never fought on its soil."

Elisabeth took hold of his hand. "But I would miss you, Georg. So would my siblings. And then there's Eva, and your child! And with your father now... Your family needs you." Georg had become an anchor in Elisabeth's life, someone she relied on to help her no matter what. His words comforted her and encouraged her when she had no one else to speak to about her troubles. He couldn't leave! Not now, not ever.

Georg finally raised his gaze. "I hope one day you realize just how special a soul you really are, Lissika." He tapped the burned edge of his cigarette and the ashes floated to the ground, where he crushed them once more. "But to have my family look at me as they do...?" He shook his head. "I also envy Samuel for his life on the *salasch*. But I can't move the forge without great effort, and even if I did, bringing everything into town from a workshop out there would be too difficult. With my father on his deathbed, I have to continue with the blacksmithing alone. I'll never find an apprentice: fathers won't trust me to teach their sons."

Footsteps alerted them both to someone approaching. Georg pushed himself against a post, fear on his face. Elisabeth had noticed behaviour like this before but didn't have the courage to ask about it.

It was Eva. "Lissika? Have you seen—?" Eva's hands flew to her cheeks. "Georg! Are you all right? What happened? Another one?" She rushed to her husband and began trying to brush the dirt off him only to realize how useless her efforts would be.

Georg's voice was small. "I'm sorry. I tried to come here before anyone saw."

"At least you weren't in the workshop. What would have happened if you...?" Eva left the question hanging, and Elisabeth didn't allow herself to imagine how it might end.

Georg didn't make eye contact with his wife. Eva was a kind woman, and Elisabeth had seen her grow in understanding as time passed. But that was obviously not enough comfort for him. The sadness of the war always hung over their family like a storm cloud.

"I'll get you some clean clothes," Eva said, and disappeared.

Georg threw his cigarette in the trough, and its tip sizzled as it sank. "I hate it here."

"Where would you go?"

He shrugged. "Somewhere in America. I can farm and forge. I've heard they're looking for men who can work. I can't stay here. I'm told I can't go in to visit my father because seeing me will upset him."

How could a family forbid their oldest son from seeing his sick father? Shivers ran down Elisabeth's spine as she realized the depths of disdain his family had for him. If her family didn't want her, Elisabeth wondered if she, too, would want to move far away.

Elisabeth and Georg noticed the sniffles and quiet sobbing of a child and looked in that direction.

"Rosina...?" Elisabeth said softly.

Her head hanging and hands clasped in front of her, Rosina stepped into the stalls from the entrance. Half of Elisabeth was angry at her sister for hiding. How much had she heard? But the other half pitied her: Elisabeth and Georg had spoken about things a child Rosina's age should not know about.

Rosina rushed to Georg, her arms outstretched, but Elisabeth caught her before she flattened herself against

Georg's dirty body. "You can't leave," Rosina said through her sobs. "Tata's already gone. You can't leave, too."

Georg patted Rosina's head. "But your father is coming home soon. Then you won't need me anymore."

Rosina burst into a wail and wrapped her arms around Elisabeth. If she had been taller, she would have squeezed the air out of her oldest sister. Elisabeth returned the embrace but motioned to Georg to help comfort her, too.

He stepped closer and rubbed Rosina's back as he lowered himself to one knee beside her.

"I didn't mean to upset you, Little Rosi."

Rosina let go of Elisabeth and wiped her nose with the back of her hand. "Little Rosi?"

Elisabeth reminded her sister about the handkerchief in her skirt pocket, but Rosina's chest still heaved as she tried to calm down. Georg reached it for her and dabbed at the wet streaks running down her face.

"Is it all right that I call you that?"

Rosina's eyes lit up, and she nodded her head so much Elisabeth worried it would fall off. How did children change moods so fast?

"Now my name is different from my cousin's!" There was a Rosina on Mammi's side of the family, too.

Georg tucked Rosina's handkerchief back in her pocket and Rosina became serious again, even faster than Mammi on a bad day. "But you can't leave us." Her mouth turned upside down, and Elisabeth feared another outburst.

Georg placed his hands on her shoulders. "Do you ever have bad dreams that scare you so much that you wake up?"

Rosina nodded.

"I have those every day, Little Rosi. Sometimes they even happen when I'm awake."

"Is that why people make fun of you?"

"Rosina!" Elisabeth scolded. "You don't ask such questions!" She tried to apologize to Georg, but he held up his hand to say it was all right.

Turning back to Rosina, he nodded. "I believe that if I live somewhere else, where no one knows me, my life will be easier. Then I won't have so many nightmares." He stood up and brushed off his knees.

Eva had still not returned. *She's probably trying to bring out his clothes without anyone seeing*, Elisabeth thought. With the household as busy as it was, she didn't blame her.

Rosina whimpered. "But this is your home. You can't leave your home."

"We all need you," Elisabeth said. "Even with Tata home. We will find a way to help you."

Georg shook his head. "There's no way to help me, Lissika. There are thousands of men like me in this country, and no one helps us. The war was lost, our empire broken into pieces. Soldiers are suffering everywhere and can't get help."

"But they don't have us as their family," Rosina said through sniffles.

Georg lowered himself to Rosina's level again and placed both hands on her cheeks. "Lukas-Bátschi's children are all so special." A big sigh signalled to Elisabeth that he was holding back his own tears. "You're right. They don't have you as their family. I'm very lucky that I do."

CHAPTER SEVENTEEN

After a couple hours of studying, followed by family lunch where Juliana said nothing to Opa about the photos, Mom and Opa went outside to tend to the flower beds. Opa wasn't much of a gardener—he'd once told Juliana how he thought it funny that everyone was into gardening these days, while he preferred to put his feet up and watch television. But Mom had convinced him to come and enjoy the sun.

Juliana took advantage of the quiet time to inspect the photo drawer in the wall unit in the living room. She'd searched in there once before. Many of the photos appeared to be of her mom's family several decades ago: she recognized Uncle Peter's flashy smile, Mom's scowls at her older sister, and Aunt Anne's take-charge posture. But many were filled with strangers, too.

Juliana pushed aside a package with photos from a family camping trip and gasped. A black-and-white photo stuck out of a small envelope, with the kerchiefed head of a woman at its centre. She lifted the photo out and studied it. The woman's age was a mystery—black-and-white photos could hide age well. But Juliana recalled what Opa had told her once: only older, married women dressed in black from head to toe. Young married women sometimes still wore colourful clothes for their Sunday best, but once they passed some magical age where they likely wouldn't remarry, they wore black. Juliana had learned that "older" back then meant after thirty. She tried to picture Mom in these traditional costumes and laughed.

In another photo, a woman sat in a chair in what might have been a photo studio, judging by the curtain behind her, with a younger woman standing beside her, her hand on the older woman's shoulder. The younger woman's kerchief, blouse, shawl, skirt, and socks were all various shades of grey. Juliana wondered what the true colours had been.

"I'd love to share these with Sophie," she mused aloud. Her cousin seemed to be the only one somewhat interested in these stories. "But will showing them to her make her uncomfortable?"

"What do you mean?"

Juliana jumped. She hadn't heard Dad coming. "What?"

"I asked, what do you mean? What will make who uncomfortable?"

Juliana needed a moment to collect herself. Only through Dad's interruption did she realize how lost she'd become in her search. She wished Elisabeth were a photographer instead of a visual artist, but Juliana also understood how unreasonable that wish was, given the time period. Even with her limited knowledge of world history, she knew cameras weren't exactly available at every corner store.

If there were even corner stores.

"Sophie. She has special glasses that help her see, but she's too embarrassed to wear them, even when it's just the two of us."

Dad knelt on the carpet next to Juliana and looked through the photos. Juliana picked up a few more and saw glimpses of trees, white house walls, and horses in the background. Everyone was posed in each photo showing that photos were obviously very special back then.

"They didn't have smartphones, that's for sure," she said.

"Nope," Dad answered. He eyed a few of Mom as a teen and smiled. A moment later, his eyes flashed a little mischief as he plucked one from the drawer and showed it to Juliana. "And she's just as adorable now."

Juliana wrinkled her nose. "Oh my god, Dad, just don't." *Yuck.*

Dad laughed. "That never gets old. But those are wonderful photos. Too bad they're just thrown in there like that." Pressing down on the coffee table behind him, Dad stood up and sat on the couch. "My legs are getting too old to kneel for that long. So, Sophie feels left out, I guess?"

Juliana set the photos in her hands back into the drawer, closed it, and turned around to face Dad. "I get it. Aunt Anne showed me a picture of them on her phone: they've got these tiny telescope-like lenses attached to what look like regular glasses. I wouldn't want to wear them at school either, especially if I was getting bullied."

Dad's neck and shoulders tightened. "Someone's bullying her?"

"A couple of girls."

"That's disgusting. And let me guess: the school has a zero-tolerance policy for bullying."

Juliana nodded. "They all do."

Dad sighed. "That explains why she won't wear those glasses even in front of you."

Juliana leaned onto the coffee table. "But why not? Doesn't she trust me? I'm not those girls. I'd never make fun of her."

"I know. And so does your mom, and so do your aunt and uncles. And I'm certain that Sophie trusts you, too. But deep down, she's probably really scared. When I was both your ages, my parents moved around a lot, because they kept getting kicked out of wherever we were renting."

Juliana sat up straight. "You've never told me that before." Her tone was soft, not accusing.

Dad leaned back into the couch and crossed his ankle over his knee. The air in the room shifted, and Juliana realized Dad was trying to figure out how to say something that made him uncomfortable. These moments happened so rarely that she didn't recognize it at first, and they certainly didn't happen when he was on the road.

"Your mom and I chose not to tell you much about my family when you were young, because it's not a background we thought you'd understand. But you're old enough now, and I'm home to actually tell you." He tugged on his shirt while he collected his thoughts. "My mom came from a rough background. Drugs were a normal thing for her. From what I was told, she abstained while she was pregnant with me, but she started up again when I was too young to remember her sober. My dad came from a decent family, but when he returned from Vietnam, he couldn't stay in a country that supported that kind of war."

Juliana cocked her head. "Your dad was American?"

He nodded.

"I'm...a quarter American? That's kind of cool. So, what happened? I mean, I don't see anything wrong with that. He didn't like war and came here. So what?"

"He came here after he saw the photo of Phan Thi Kim Phuc running from a napalm attack in Vietnam." At Juliana's confused expression, he pulled out his phone.

"You've likely seen it, you just don't recognize the name." In a matter of moments, his tiny screen showed a black-and-white picture of a naked Vietnamese girl screaming as she and others ran down a road. It was a stark contrast to the poised photos she had just seen of Tata's family. It sent shivers down her spine.

Dad tucked his phone away. "My father had terrible experiences in the war—I'll spare you the details. When he saw that photo—whenever that was—he knew he couldn't live in a country that supported that. So he fled here."

"Is that how he met your mom—Grandma? What do I call her?"

Dad waved his hand, and Juliana was surprised at his apparent lack of caring. "She wouldn't have been a grand-mother to you, anyway. She was living near the American border in Alberta when she met him and agreed to marry him so he could legally stay in the country. But over the years, her drug addiction took hold and Dad had to get a restraining order to keep her away from us. All the years he was trying to raise me, though, his PTSD would show up—shouting at me, calling me an idiot for not knowing how to tie my shoes, that sort of thing." He took a deep breath. Juliana clenched her jaw. "He loved me—I could see it in his eyes—but he couldn't deal with the demons in his mind. When he heard that Canada had entered into war in Somalia in the Nineties, he knew families would be killed again, and he feared seeing pictures like that in the paper and on the news." Dad wiped tears off his cheeks. "It brought it all back. He took his own life."

Juliana's eyes became wet and she sniffled. She had thought something was wrong with her father because he was hovering, because he had turned into some kind of control freak. Yes, something was wrong with him, but it was that he didn't have...real parents, at least not the way she had parents. Sure, Dad had been on the road most of her life, but she could call him, and they talked—sometimes shouted, to be honest—when he was home. Their relationship had been rocky for the past few years, but now, in this living room, at this moment, the shifts in the air turned into a shift in their relationship.

"I'm so sorry, Dad. I had no idea. Can I ask what happened to your mom?"

Dad grabbed a tissue from the box on the coffee table and blew his nose. "She died in 2002 of a drug overdose."

If there was one thing she was learning in Kitchener, it was that people are who they are because of the people who came before them, like a factory conveyor belt, where everyone on the line adds to the object travelling along it.

"So," Dad continued, "that's why I find this parenting thing so difficult. I know my parents tried the best they could, but it was hard to learn from that."

Juliana smiled. "Actually, Dad, I think I can help with that..."

Dad raised an eyebrow.

JULIANA CLICKED to the next slide. The heading read, "Teenager Dress Code." On the slide were images of young women from different centuries in a range of outfits: white wigs and hoop skirts, elaborate dresses that hugged the bodice but flowed to ankle length, and perfect perms and shoulder-padded sweaters atop jeans.

Dad cracked up before Juliana could even introduce the slide. "Okay, okay, I get the dress code thing!" He couldn't say more than that. Laughing, Juliana moved to the next slide.

She was about halfway through her presentation on parenting a teen. At the start, her stomach had felt like it had just finished an hour of acrobatics class, but now she and Dad were having a blast. Although he did protest at a few pointers—such as morning routines sometimes being inefficient—he listened to much of what Juliana said.

The side door opened and in walked Opa, Mom, Aunt Anne, and Uncle Peter.

Opa had a huge smile on his face. "Look who came by!"

As everyone took off their shoes on the landing, Uncle Peter said, "The weather was so nice, I thought I'd just drop by because, you know, I live in town now." He flashed his cheesy grin.

Aunt Anne patted her younger brother's arm. "It's great to have you back."

Opa beamed. "The four of us pulled all the weeds at the front and trimmed the flowers. Now everyone who lives in the apartment building across the street has a nice house to look at."

Juliana tried to disconnect her laptop from the television before they entered the kitchen, but her fingers couldn't latch on to the cables fast enough.

"No, no, leave this," Mom said, grinning. "Are you getting parenting lessons?"

Opa and his children broke out into laughter while Dad turned red.

"Very funny," Dad said. "But as a matter of fact, yes, I am, and you should listen. I'll bet you'd learn a few things."

Aunt Anne crossed her arms and raised an eyebrow. "Oh, really? Well then. After raising four teenagers already, I wonder what it is you think I have to learn." Uncle Peter leaned against the kitchen sink while the rest sat at the table.

"Continue, Jules," Dad said.

Now Juliana's cheeks turned the colour of strawberries. This wasn't exactly what she had planned. "Um, okay."

Opa stared at the television. "What kind of show is this?"

"It's not a show, Tata," Mom answered. "Juliana is giving Paul a presentation on how to parent teenagers. She's connected her laptop to the TV so the picture is bigger."

Opa's eyes popped open wide. "You can do that now?" Everyone nodded. "*Na so was.*"

Juliana didn't understand the German, but judging by the expression on his face and his tone of voice, it was something you said when you were surprised.

"It's too bad we couldn't do this a long time ago. You could have taught Georg. He was a horrible father."

Dad's back stiffened and the air in the room turned thick.

Temptation pulled words out of Juliana's mouth. "So you knew Georg?"

The joy on Opa's face vanished. "I never met him." Opa headed to his bedroom in the basement without uttering another word.

Mom, Aunt Anne, and Uncle Peter stared at Juliana. Juliana looked at Dad for help. He told her it would be okay to explain what she knew.

Juliana unplugged her laptop from the television and inserted the adapter into her phone.

"Georg?" Aunt Anne said. "The man you were asking about?"

"Now that I think of it," Mom said, "you've mentioned his name to me before." She looked at her siblings. "But no one's ever told us about him, right?"

Uncle Peter and Aunt Anne shook their heads.

Juliana tapped her phone a few times, and a moment

later the photo she had taken in Claire's Tea Shop was broadcast to the television.

"See that man with the cigarette?" Everyone nodded. "That's Georg."

"Are you sure?" Mom asked.

Juliana ran to her room, got the pictures from the factory Uncle Peter had given her, her notebook on Schuhmacher family history, and Elisabeth's sketchbook. Back in the kitchen, she opened everything and pointed out the similarities between Elisabeth's drawings and the photos and confirmed that Claire had called him George Shoemaker.

After giving everyone a moment to study the images, Dad asked, "And you're certain the three of you never met him?"

Mom shook her head. "The story is that our parents immigrated first to Pennsylvania and then came here a year later. Right?" She looked to her siblings for confirmation, and they nodded.

Peter stroked his chin. "When you think about it, it seems a bit unbelievable that Tata and Modr were allowed to immigrate to the States first and then Canada. I mean, the paperwork alone would've taken longer than one year to process... The paperwork!" He rushed to the stairs. "Juliana, come with me. I know where the immigration documents are."

As Uncle Peter and Juliana reached the basement, Opa's television blared the news broadcast from behind his closed bedroom door.

"Are you sure we should be doing this?" Juliana asked. "I just keep making him angry anytime I bring it up."

They entered the rec room and then the cellar.

"I don't want to make Tata angry either, but I want to learn the truth about our family. Despite all my travels, it never occurred to me that the immigration story might not be what we were told."

To Juliana's knowledge, only she and Sophie had been in the cellar since Oma had died. She shuddered as she remembered how disgusting it had been when she first discovered it. Although the two girls had cleaned it while searching for that funny dance photo of Mom, that had been several months ago, which meant no one had cleaned it since. Although the dust was far less thick than it had been that day in December when she had run in here to escape the changes in her life, dust still flew as Uncle Peter moved boxes. She sneezed into her arm.

"Here we go." Uncle Peter set a newer-looking box on top of a pile of older ones. On the side it said, "Papers." He pulled open the flaps, and a spider crawled out. Juliana shrieked and Uncle Peter laughed. "Don't worry, it won't land in your hair." Mischief danced in his eyes.

Juliana shot him a look.

Uncle Peter smiled and shrugged. "Couldn't help it. The older guys at the factory ribbed a lot. Guess some of it wore off on me." He pulled out several envelopes until he found the one he wanted. "This is it. The immigration papers. I helped Tata organize things after Modr died and remembered seeing this envelope. But since I knew the story—or thought I knew it—I didn't bother reading these in any detail." He opened the enclosure and then stopped. "I'll do this upstairs in front of the others. Let's go."

As they entered the kitchen, Uncle Peter held up the envelope while Juliana bounced up and down and shook out her hands to release some of the energy. Dad gave her a knowing smile, and she smiled back.

"What does it say?" Aunt Anne asked.

Uncle Peter slid the papers out and spread them on the table. Everyone leaned in and gently pawed at them as they shifted the papers about to read them.

Within moments, everyone gasped: the papers were dated for the year Opa and Oma had arrived in North America, only they had come directly to Canada. They'd been sponsored.

By George Shoemaker.

Mom's jaw dropped open. "What on earth?"

"Are we reading this right?" Aunt Anne asked.

Dad answered. "Given that all five of us are reading the

same papers and have come to the same conclusion, I'd say we are."

Mom picked up Tata's immigration form. "By why lie about this? I mean, so what if he came here first?"

Aunt Anne parked her hands on her hips. "Tata's always saying about how family should support each other. Obviously this George—Georg—was family and supported Tata and Modr. So why...?"

"I want answers," Mom said. She and Aunt Anne exchanged glances and nodded; that sister thing Juliana wished she had with someone. They said in unison, "Peter."

Peter clapped his hand to his chest. "Me? Why me?"

"You're the peacekeeper," Mom said.

Aunt Anne added, "And you spent all those summers with him in the factory. There's a father-son bond that the two of us just don't have with him."

Uncle Peter began protesting, but Juliana pushed him toward the stairs, causing everyone to laugh despite the seriousness of the truth they were seeking.

CHAPTER EIGHTEEN

Stefan held the bucket of clothespins while keeping his back to the clothesline. Elisabeth lifted a wet underskirt from her laundry basket, threw the waist over the line, smoothed it out, and pinned it in place.

"Rosina," she called to her sister. "You missed a few weeds by the lettuce. Please pull those out."

Rosina scowled, but obeyed. As much as Elisabeth disliked how Rosina acted toward her, she also felt a little relieved: Rosina's actions suggested that yesterday hadn't upset her too much.

Elisabeth turned her attention back to Stefan. "How are things at Margarethe-Néni's house?"

"Not well. I haven't seen Georg this bad. He's pale, tired, sometimes confused. And Eva..."

Elisabeth shared yesterday's events with Stefan. Then

she lowered her voice. "I had no idea Rosina cared for Georg so much. If he leaves, not only will he be hurting his wife and unborn child but also us."

Stefan shook his head in sadness. "I wish I could help him more."

"I can't believe there's nothing we can do."

Stefan rested his arm for a moment before holding the bucket up for Elisabeth again, his back still turned to the laundry line.

"You can put that on the ground, if you'd like," Elisabeth said.

Stefan smiled at her. "Then I wouldn't be of much help to you, and your mother would ask me to leave." He faced away again.

Elisabeth's cheeks blushed. She pulled out another underskirt from the basket.

"He feels alone here," Stefan said. "I don't know how to describe it. He's surrounded by people but he's still alone."

Elisabeth had thought that, too, and she didn't have a word for it either. Georg lived with his parents and wife, worked alongside Samuel and sometimes Stefan at the *salasch*, attended church... He was rarely alone, and yet he had very few people who actually wanted him in their lives. Even his father was pushing him away at a time he needed his oldest son the most.

"If he moves across the ocean," Stefan continued, "it'll be worse. He'll feel alone and sad *and* he won't have people like us and your siblings around to keep him company. That can destroy a man."

Rosina stood up from gardening. "Is Georg going to get better? Should I knit him a scarf?"

This was the good heart that was inside each of her siblings, and Elisabeth thought it strange that a man like Georg could arouse fear in so many people but compassion in her siblings and herself. For all the talk of forgiveness in church, the community had a funny way of practising it, selecting only people they liked as recipients of their forgiveness. It angered Elisabeth.

She hung up a third underskirt as she answered Rosina's question. "What about making him a salad? It's summer and you still take a long time to knit. You haven't finished your own scarf yet, remember?"

Rosina bit on her bottom lip as she thought about Elisabeth's suggestion. "Cookies! They're more special."

Elisabeth shook her head. "I didn't plan to bake today, so the oven isn't ready."

"Then how about tomorrow? My cookies will make him happy."

Elisabeth smiled at the comment. In truth, she would be doing most of the baking, but she didn't mind if her sister took credit.

Something was changing inside Rosina after all. The youngest Schumacher child often offered to make things for people, but those previous requests had come from a place of self-importance. Yes, she was going to tell Georg that she had baked the cookies, but Rosina was open to other ideas this time. She didn't get angry when Elisabeth mentioned the scarf that, at its current length, would cover one shoulder. Nor did she fight back when Elisabeth pointed out the difficulties with the oven—she would need to get cornstalk out of the cow stalls and begin a fire, then wait for some time before the oven was hot enough. Yes, Rosina had replied with anger when Elisabeth pointed out a few missed weeds, but not when she was trying to help someone. In other words, this idea wasn't about Rosina: she really did want to do something that would make Georg happy.

"Could Anna help, then?" Elisabeth asked. "I'm sure she'd like to help our cousin feel better, too. I saw how sad she was when you told her last night what had happened."

Rosina nodded. "And Luki said he wants to help, too, maybe make Georg a pair of shoes. I know Mammi won't let him, and Luki can't bake because he's a boy. But he wants to do something."

Elisabeth exchanged smiles with Stefan. Her youngest sister had indeed thought of everyone. "But first, we must get ahead in our chores so we have time tomorrow to bake those cookies."

Rosina rushed back to the garden and, with the focus of an eagle on its prey, tore out every weed, and only weeds.

"That was remarkable," Stefan said, keeping his voice

low. "I expected an outburst from her because of your suggestions."

Elisabeth quickly hung up a few pairs of socks, knowing she would need to sew today to make room for baking tomorrow.

"I was worried how yesterday would affect her. You should have heard her when Georg said he wanted to leave. I never thought my sister's cries would pull at my heart as they did. She was truly scared."

"Speaking of which, I should get going, too. I'll stop by Georg's on my way to the church and then visit him again on my way home," he said. "If you find a little time this afternoon to help Georg and Eva—Herr Schuhmacher has lots of help—I think they would like that."

Rosina had overheard him. "But what about the cookies? We can't bake them today."

Stefan walked over to her and gave her a hug. "Georg tells me he now calls you Little Rosi." Rosina nodded. "You may be little but you have a big heart. No matter when you bake your cookies, I'm certain Georg will be happy."

Elisabeth promised both that she would do her best, and she meant it.

After Stefan left, Elisabeth took a moment to pray, again asking why Georg had to suffer so, but again she did not receive an answer. She finished her prayer by asking if Jesus could at least protect Georg and his family from further tragedy.

Elisabeth checked on Rosina's work. "You're doing a very good job. You haven't pulled out a single vegetable yet. Very nice!"

Despite the compliment, Rosina scowled again. "Leave me alone."

Taken aback by her sister's unexpected anger, Elisabeth was about to admonish her for her rude words when the gate at the front of the property creaked open. Mammi had returned from Margarethe-Néni's house.

Mammi stared at the ground as she walked slowly toward the house rather than in her usual proud, confident way.

Mammi looked tired and it wasn't even lunchtime yet: she had spent only one hour at the other Schuhmacher household. Even when Mammi used to be in charge of her own family's day-to-day duties, Elisabeth could not remember a time when she seemed this exhausted by mid-morning.

As Mammi neared her daughters, Elisabeth saw she was as white as Stefan had described Georg. Elisabeth rushed to her to offer her an arm, but Mammi swatted it away.

"Are you all right?" After Mammi's miscarriage several months ago, any time Mammi looked pale, Elisabeth worried she was sick again.

Mammi remained silent until she reached the summer

kitchen, where she dropped onto the bench. "Fetch me some water, bread, butter, and cheese."

"Me, too!" Rosina added.

"If you want something, you can help your sister," Mammi said. "Have I taught you nothing? You should never be a burden on your family."

Rosina jumped up and followed Elisabeth to the kitchen inside the house. When they returned, their hands full, they found Mammi resting her head on the table.

"Mammi?" Elisabeth said gently. Mammi seemed to have aged thirty years but she raised her head and sat up. "Are you sure you're all right?"

Rosina sat at the other end of the table, her eyes fixed on Mammi. Elisabeth guessed she, too, was scared by this uncommon sight. Most of the time, their mother was either angry or stern. If she was happy, the corners of her mouth might turn up only a little: Mammi believed one looked stupid with a smile. If she was tired, she immediately went to bed, but that never happened until night. If she was sick, she forced herself to keep working until she could no longer stand. But then, too, she would go to bed.

Pale, tired, and eating was a condition Elisabeth was unfamiliar with.

Mammi drank the cup of water in one gulp and asked for more. When Elisabeth returned with more water, Mammi had already eaten half her food. Her colour was returning, but her tiredness remained.

Rosina was still sitting at her end of the table, chewing slower than a cow, her eyes not leaving their mother.

"I have been a pious woman all my life." Mammi stared at her plate as she spoke. "God punishes—we are taught that through the Bible and Luther's words—but he does not torture." Mammi took another bite of her food, and Elisabeth thought it best not to interrupt. "Konrad will not look at anyone, not even Margarethe. His pride has been stolen by this stroke. Why would God let him suffer like this? Either take his life and be done with it or give him back the life he had before this happened." Mammi ate a little more.

Elisabeth disliked her uncle for many reasons, least of all for how he treated his oldest son. But she took no joy in his sickness either.

Mammi held out her cup. "Get me more water."

Elisabeth obeyed. When she gave Mammi her glass back, she was relieved to see even more colour in her face. Rosina must have noticed, too, for she ate faster now.

"Is there anything else I can get you?" Elisabeth asked.

Mammi didn't answer right away, and Elisabeth didn't know whether to repeat the question in case Mammi hadn't heard. But noticing that her mouth was full, Elisabeth waited.

Mammi sighed. "I was at Margarethe's for an hour. In that time, Georg had two fits."

Rosina's mouth gaped and her eyes welled up.

Elisabeth rushed to sit next to her and rubbed her back. "Stefan was here just before you left and said he's been having them more often."

Mammi nodded. "We passed each other, but I was too tired to greet him." She picked up a slice of cheese, looked at it, and set it back down. "Georg's second fit was in the workshop, near the forge. The fire over the coals was blue. He was screaming, telling my brother to get down before someone shot him." Mammi's eyes turned red.

"Do you mean Andreas-Bátschi?" Elisabeth asked.

"Georg was terrified. I have never seen that kind of look in a man's eyes."

To Elisabeth's knowledge, Georg had not seen Mammi's brother get shot; he had only found him afterwards, in the field hospital, dying of his wounds. Something was creating these nightmares for him.

"Andreas-Bátschi? Who is that?" Rosina's question surprised Elisabeth until she realized that Rosina was far too young to remember either of Mammi's brothers. Elisabeth asked her to return to weeding. Her temper flaring, Rosina shouted that she would not.

Mammi glared at her youngest. "Your sister has asked you to do your chores. Listen to her or you can kneel in a box of corn."

Rosina's glare reminded Elisabeth of a pitchfork. Saying nothing more, Rosina stomped all the way to the vegetable garden.

"She is too young for this," Mammi said. "What she learned yesterday was not for her ears." She returned to the topic at hand. "Yes, Andreas. The fear and panic in his eyes, Lissika... I have no choice but to believe now that he loved my brother like his own." Mammi took a handkerchief from her skirt pocket and dabbed her eyes. "I didn't want to leave him but I am not strong enough to help a man the size of Georg in such a state. I shouted for Schubkegel Adam, and he brought Wagner Michael." She shook her head. "They had to fight Georg to pull him away from the forge, and I don't believe Georg even knew he was fighting his brothers-in-law. He was so close to the fire, and I am certain all three men have bruises. Samuel came in not much later with a bucket of water and doused the coals, but the other men had not yet pushed Georg outside. When the water hit the coals, Georg yelled for everyone to get down. He was as terrified as a mouse about to be eaten by a cat: he believed a bomb had landed."

Elisabeth dried her eyes with her apron. Georg was living in a nightmare and waking up was nearly impossible for him. She couldn't stand here and hang up laundry while his mind disappeared.

"May I go to him?" she asked. "Maybe I can help."

To Elisabeth's relief, Mammi nodded. "I know now that what is happening to him is not God's doing. Just like God would not torture someone like Konrad, despite his self-important ways, He would also not punish any man with such horrible dreams. God is our Father: he punishes to teach, not to hurt."

Elisabeth held her breath. Had she heard right? Although Mammi had not said that she forgave Georg, nor that she had stopped blaming him for her brother's death, she agreed with Elisabeth that God was not punishing Georg.

"I will finish the laundry," Mammi said. "My customers can wait an extra day. Your father's family—all of his family—needs help, and I am too tired to go back."

Elisabeth thanked Mammi, cleared the dishes from the table, and hurried inside to pack, eating the food left on Mammi's and Rosina's plates. When she stepped out the door again, Mammi called her over.

"Yes?"

"You were planning an evening of *majen*, were you not?"

"I was going to, but—"

Mammi narrowed her eyes. "Simply answer the question."

She was returning to normal. Surprisingly, that gave Elisabeth some comfort.

"Yes," Elisabeth answered.

"Have you invited anyone?"

"No."

"Good. Instead, I want you to invite Konrad's family on Sunday. All of them. Including Georg. You may invite Stefan, too. They all need a rest."

Elisabeth grinned from ear to ear. "Thank you!"

"Wipe that smile off your face. You look stupid."

Elisabeth did as she was told, but only for as long as Mammi could see her face. Mammi was back to normal and Elisabeth could still plan something so she could prepare for when Tata returned. Not only that but she would be helping his family. She needed to meet with Maria as soon as possible; she could not make a single mistake.

"And buy some coffee," Mammi said as Elisabeth walked toward the first gate. "I will show you how to brew it. If you do it wrong, we'll never hear the end of it at church."

CHAPTER NINETEEN

Juliana had spent the last twenty minutes sharing stories about Georg, Elisabeth, and other Schuhmacher ancestors. Dad, Mom, and Aunt Anne were now examining the drawing Juliana still hadn't deciphered: the galloping horse.

"That's clearly a man's leg," Dad said.

Mom and Aunt Anne agreed.

"But from what I recall," Aunt Anne said, "they didn't ride the horse: they rode in the wagon. At least that's what the few photos I've seen over the years have shown." She looked up at Juliana. "You're welcome to look at them any time. I know Tata has a bunch in that drawer, but the few that struck me somehow are in a photo album in our house so they wouldn't get ruined. I don't know much about them; I just liked them. Maybe you'll be able to figure out a thing or two."

Juliana thanked her aunt and promised to spend more time in the summer investigating the photographs. To say that learning about her great-grandmother had given her the strength to adjust to this move was an understatement.

"My guess is that someone who rides on a horse would have been in the cavalry," Dad said. "Georg fought in the war. Is this him?"

It sounded plausible.

"But if that's him," Juliana said, "why is he in such a rush?"

Before anyone guessed an answer, they heard the sound of footsteps on the basement stairs and turned to face the doorway. Uncle Peter entered first, followed by Opa.

Juliana closed all the books out of fear that something would upset Opa, but the gentle smile on his face as he sat down at the table comforted her. Whatever Uncle Peter had said, Opa's anger had—at least for the moment—disappeared.

"You are stubborn like your mother," Opa said to Juliana, his expression still soft. "I wish you would stop asking questions, but I can see that's very hard for you."

Juliana remained standing by the television. Her cheeks burned and she stared at the ground. "I'm really sorry, Opa. It's just that Elisabeth drew so many pictures of Georg. When I suspected he was here, I couldn't stop." She glanced up, a sheepish smile on her face. "He kind of became like a famous person to me."

Opa smiled and nodded. "I only hope what I have to say doesn't upset you. I love my family and don't want them sad or angry with me. That's why I need to explain everything." He sighed and folded his hands on the table. "I don't go to church every Sunday here. But I did in Semlak. The pastor always taught us that God wants us to be honest, but I even made Irmgard promise to keep this a secret. She did not agree with me, but she respected my decision."

Uncle Peter was leaning against the sink at the back of the kitchen, opposite Juliana, who stayed where she was. Between them sat Dad, Aunt Anne, and Mom at the table with Opa. Silence hung over the family, but it was different from the one at Uncle Peter's a few days before and similar to the one Juliana had experienced with Dad. Again she felt a sense of anticipation that something big was about to happen. She looked around at the others to see if they were feeling it. Uncle Peter's expression was one of compassion, Aunt Anne's one of confusion, and Mom's one of mild anger. But Dad's face was blank. What was he thinking?

"The dictatorship in Romania ruined everything," Opa began. "We couldn't travel except to other Communist countries. We didn't own a home. And if you spoke out against the regime, you were punished. I wanted me and Irmgard to immigrate to Pennsylvania where my grandfather had worked after the First World War. I knew I would find descendants from Semlak there and so I might find a little piece of home in a new country." He took a deep breath. "Life after the Second World War was very, very hard. When Mammi returned with me to Semlak—I think I was three years old—she moved in with Anni-Néni, and Eva joined us soon after. Mammi forced her to because Eva was so sad. She had lost two sons to the war, and her daughter came back from a Russian camp a few years after the war. Many died there, but I do not wish to talk about that."

Juliana didn't want to press Opa with other difficult topics. She would simply look it up later.

Opa continued. "Two other sons were always in trouble with the law. Eva had no man in the house to help her, and she needed a man. But Georg wasn't dead, so she couldn't remarry. And they did not divorce." He stared at his hands. "As I grew up, I saw how Mammi, Anni-Néni, and Eva helped each other." He interlaced his fingers and gently shook his hands at Juliana. "They were very close, Yulika. Like this. They lost so much, and Georg, who lived here, did not. He did not support his family, and he left them to survive the Second World War on their own."

"That's why you don't like him," Juliana said.

Opa nodded. "No man should *ever* leave his family behind."

Juliana better understood Opa's opinion about Georg now, but through her conversations with Dad, she also understood Georg's side of the story. Or rather, she believed she did. Who was right? Was there even a right solution to this?

"As you know, Yulika, Georg let these fits take over his mind. Mammi tried to explain to me all the time what a good man he was, but all I saw was a person—not a man—who had left his family behind."

Dad sucked in his breath—a sign he was getting angry—and his hands turned into fists on his lap. The muscles in his jaw rippled, but he said nothing. Juliana had never seen him try to repress his feelings like this before. He usually yelled at her—sometimes Mom, too—if he was angry. If he tried to calm himself down, he would leave the room.

Opa continued, oblivious to Dad's reaction. "From what Mammi and Eva told me, Georg fled to Canada in the Thirties. Eva and their family didn't join him, because they believed he would come home in a few years, like my *otata* had maybe fifteen years earlier. They said that Georg saw the war with Germany coming and that his fits about the first war had become worse."

Dad locked eyes with Opa. "He believed his options were suicide or flight, Peter."

Opa kept eye contact with Dad and sat up straighter. "That's what family is for: to help you."

"Family can't always help you in situations like that."

"Then what is family for?"

Silence fell over the family. Mom took hold of Dad's

hand, and the looks they exchanged told Juliana that Mom knew about Dad's family, too.

Opa continued. "Family is there to support you, no matter what. Mammi told me stories, sad stories, about how they tried to help Georg for years. Why did he not change? It is clear he didn't want to."

"It's much more complicated than that," Dad said. "*Much* more complicated. You're talking about a soldier who witnessed unmentionable horrors during that war. World War One made its mark on history in part because of the carnage." At Opa's confused look, Dad explained, "Because of how many people died. So many countries were involved that millions had to fight."

Opa shrugged. "In Romania we only learned about how Russia saved everyone."

Juliana was already looking up the statistic on her phone. "This website says that thirty nations fought in World War One." Thirty countries? She reported more facts. "The war happened all over Europe. There was a Western Front, and an Eastern one...and one in Southeast Europe. But the war was also fought in Africa and the Middle East." She paused and then gasped. "They estimate that sixteen million people—soldiers and civilians—were killed. That's almost half of Canada!"

"Today," Dad said. "What was the population of Canada in 1918?"

Juliana searched it up. "About eight million. So twice our population back then died in one war."

Dad nodded. "In trench warfare, dead bodies might lie next to you in the mud, or if you had to attack, you ran over dead bodies in No Man's Land... I have no idea how any man came out of that sane, especially given the lack of mental health awareness back then."

Opa stared at the table for a minute or two but said nothing.

Juliana's stomach turned into knots. The only bits she had learned about the World Wars were from her teachers during preparation for Remembrance Day each November. She wouldn't learn twentieth-century history until Grade Ten. She knew they were called the World Wars for a reason—lots of countries were involved—but that was about it. Thirty countries? Sixteen million dead? And that was just the First World War.

Uncle Peter added, "Think about it. The most killing these men had probably done before the war was a few pigs and cows every fall. Fighting a war like that would be very traumatic for anyone."

Aunt Anne agreed. "And sixteen million dead meant sixteen million families affected."

Mom shook her head in amazement. "Probably more, actually. One man could have been a father, brother, son, uncle, cousin... They all died in combat. The civilians were simply in the way when the front came through their villages and cities." She took Opa's hand in hers. "There was no straightforward answer for Georg and Eva, Tata. World War One traumatized him, and from what you're saying, World War Two traumatized her. And had either one moved to be with the other, that trauma would have been much, much worse. Georg would have been faced with his memories repeatedly in Romania, and Eva would have been torn from the only friends she had left if she moved to Canada."

The room fell silent. Juliana's heart broke for these cousins, now ghosts in her family history.

"That means," she said, "that war kept Georg and Eva apart. It separated them precisely from the people who would have helped them the most. War destroyed their family."

Opa rubbed the top of his head and let out a heavy sigh. "This is why you must go to school, Yulika. It makes you smart. In all these years, I have never thought of it like this."

"Did Georg and Eva ever see each other again?" she asked.

He nodded. "Georg visited Semlak in the Sixties. That was the first time I saw him and..." He picked at a loose thread on the cream tablecloth. "I am ashamed now, but the truth..."

Mom laid a hand on Opa's shoulder. "Tata, if it's too

painful, you don't have to." She looked at everyone else. "Right?"

Opa shook his head. "I promised you the truth." He placed his hands flat on the table and sat up straight. He looked his family in the eyes as he spoke. "By the time I met him, I hated him. You know I do not use that word often. When I saw his fits, I believed they were his fault. I did everything possible to not speak to him while he was there."

Dad's shoulders relaxed, and he crossed his arms on the table and leaned forward. The tension in his voice from earlier had disappeared. "Do you know what was probably happening when he had those 'fits'?"

Opa shook his head. "I didn't care back then. Please tell me."

"We call them hallucinations today. He was probably reliving the war. His mind may have even made up some of his hallucinations, creating events that never took place. It would've been like being stuck in a TV horror show he couldn't turn off."

Opa sighed. "Like the pictures I have sometimes in my mind but mine are of my mother being alive." He turned to Juliana. "There is nothing worse than holding on to anger for so many years. Never do that."

Juliana wiped tears from her eyes. This entire story about Georg and Eva was so tragic...they loved each other but couldn't be together. "I won't, Opa."

Opa picked up the photo of him, Karl, and Georg and studied it, his face remaining serious. "We took this photo on my first day of work at the factory. Karl had to convince me to take it, and I said I would if he stood between me and Georg. I had done my duty and thanked him when we arrived in Canada. I did so again when he found me work. There was nothing more to say to him. It was hard for me to stand there, but this way, Anni-Néni and Eva knew we were all okay, and that was most important to me."

He paused for a moment and then looked at his grown children. "God also asks us not to judge others, but it's very hard. Irmgard and Georg wrote letters to each other when we still lived in Romania. She had almost all the paperwork ready before she told me because she knew I would not accept help from him. And yet he found me a place to work that supported my family—our family—for three generations." He sighed again. "I never told you any of this because I was too embarrassed for accepting help from such a man. But he promised my family a future in a free country and I could not refuse it. I did my duty and thanked him." He lay the photo back on the table. "Now I know it was not enough."

Uncle Peter came up behind Opa and put his arm around him. "It sounds like we have a lot to thank this man for." Then Juliana heard him say under his breath, "Especially me."

Mom and Aunt Anne must have heard him because

they moved over to Uncle Peter and each put an arm around him. Juliana knew there were countries that killed gay men and women and that people in Canada still discriminated against them. Would any of that have happened in Romania? Or would Uncle Peter have never come out? That was one question she would never ask. She wanted to learn the truth about her family, not imagine the sad possibilities that could have happened if things had gone differently.

Opa stood up. "I need to go for a walk. This has been very difficult for me." His eyes welled up. "But I hope you all understand: family is very important. I was wrong about Georg. I understand that now. But, before today, I was too embarrassed to accept help from a man who had deserted his own family when they needed him most. So embarrassed that it made me lie to my own family." He wiped his eyes and looked at Dad. "Katy told me many years ago about your father. I believed he deserted you, too. But I didn't think about what men who fight in wars see. I had to do military service in Romania when I was eighteen, but I didn't fight in a war. I see now that I was wrong about Georg and your father."

Opa held his hand out to Dad, and Dad accepted it.

"Do you want company on your walk?" Dad asked.

He shook his head. "I'm going to see Claire and look at the picture of Georg on her wall. I've always known it was there, and it was the reason I never shopped there." He again looked at Peter. "I want to make amends before..." He pointed to his head. "Before the roof damage becomes too much. Claire was always a very nice person. Very friendly. Sells very good tea."

Dad looked at everyone. "Who's Claire?"

Juliana smiled. "The lady at the tea shop. Actually, I have tea for you from her. It's supposed to help you relax so you can study better."

Dad smiled. "Let me guess. And be a good father?"

Juliana gave him a hug. "No, you already are."

CHAPTER TWENTY

It was Sunday afternoon, and the clock in the back room had struck two. Guests would arrive any moment. Rosina threw open the kitchen door and ran into the house. Elisabeth thanked Jesus that no one had been standing behind it as she closed it to keep the hot summer air out.

Rosina thrust into Elisabeth's hand a bouquet of unevenly cut, bright red poppies mixed with random weeds from the garden. "Here. I have to set out the cups." She ran to the cupboards and stacked coffee cups onto a tray.

Elisabeth watched as her youngest sibling tiptoed to the front room, the cups teetering in their piles, threatening to tip over and shatter on the loam-and-chaff floor. Rosina stared at the tray, wrinkles of worry filling her small face with each step.

Once Rosina had placed the tray on the table, Elisabeth discreetly set the weeds from the bouquet into the slop pail for the pigs. Without being asked, Anna appeared with a vase filled with water and placed the bouquet in it. She hurried to the front room and set it on the table next to the tray. Elisabeth held her breath as Rosina saw it and let it out when her sister didn't appear to notice the missing weeds.

"Can you two please get the desserts from the cellar?" she asked her sisters. They bolted for the door, prompting her to warn them: "And no eating—" The house door closed before she finished her sentence.

In the back room, Stefan was helping Luki set out shot and wine glasses for the men. Even with one arm he moved fast, appearing to finish the same number of tasks as quickly as he would have done had he had two. Luki, though, handled each glass as though it was the most delicate flower in God's kingdom. When he corrected the placement of a glass Stefan had set down, Stefan ruffled Luki's hair, prompting Luki to cry out in protest and then smooth his hair in a panic.

Elisabeth's heart fluttered and she smiled in spite of herself. She knew it was much too early to say anything to anyone, but a feeling deep inside her said Stefan would make both a good husband and a good father.

"Owa!" she cried out. Who'd pinched her?

Beside her stood Anna, laughing, a tray of cookies in her hand, and a glint of playfulness in her eyes. She and Rosina had returned quickly.

"Why are you staring at Stefan?" Anna asked Elisabeth.

Stefan, close enough to hear the question, smiled while adjusting his linen vest.

Elisabeth's cheeks burned and she punched Anna in the shoulder. "Don't embarrass me!"

Stefan let out a snort, which made Elisabeth's cheeks burn more than she thought they could. But a moment later, she broke into a smile herself. She knew he liked her, and he knew she liked him. It wasn't a secret any longer, just something one didn't talk about in front of the other person.

Or any other people, for that matter.

"Are you two working?" Mammi asked her daughters, her usual scowl on her face.

As Elisabeth grabbed a pot to boil water for coffee, she heard a knock. She barely had the house door open when all three siblings came running, forcing her to swing the pot over her head before someone slammed their face into it.

"Georg!" they shouted almost at the same time and no sooner was their cousin in the kitchen than they all hugged him. Eva's eyes glistened as she clapped her hand over her heart. Elisabeth touched her arm in comfort.

"Are you feeling better?" Anna asked.

"You won't have any nightmares here," Rosina added.

"I want to be strong like you." Luki flexed a scrawny, eight-year-old arm.

The corners of Georg's mouth turned up into a smile. He patted Anna on the head, tenderly pinched Rosina's cheek, and ruffled Luki's hair.

Luki grabbed Georg's hand and dragged him into the back room.

"Hold on there, Luki." Stefan pressed his hand to his hip, feigning indignation. "I messed your hair and you straightened it out right away. Georg does it and you don't."

"He's Georg. You're not."

That's how simple the world was, apparently.

Rosina and Anna grabbed Georg's other hand and tried to pull him back into the kitchen. Stefan, Georg, Eva, and Elisabeth all exchanged amused looks.

"I get to keep him because he's a man!" Luki told his sisters, who frowned in return. The men would all sit in the back room and the women in the front room, separated, as per custom. Anna and Rosina had no choice but to let him go.

Elisabeth, Stefan, and Eva couldn't keep their laughter hidden, and now Anna and Rosina scowled at them, too. Elisabeth told her sisters they could go play for a little until the other women came.

"Georg." Mammi placed her hands on her hips and squared herself as she faced Georg.

Elisabeth held her breath. Her mother only stood like that when she was angry, although Elisabeth had to admit that was almost all the time. Couldn't Mammi wait until after this visit? The point was to give Georg's family—all four Schuhmacher children, their spouses, and their mother if she came—a time to rest after what had happened to their father. As the host, should Elisabeth say something before Mammi ruined everything with her anger?

"As Lukas's wife," Mammi began, "it is my duty to take care of his family when I can." She paused and for the first time in a while, Elisabeth saw Mammi glance at the crucifix above the doorway to the back room. Mammi let her arms drop, and her face relaxed. She glanced at Elisabeth and then back at Georg. What was happening? Words were never a problem for Mammi. "I understand that your father's condition has caused more of your spells. Is that right?"

Georg swallowed and stared at the floor. "Yes, Lissi-Néni."

"And that you have fewer of them at the *salasch*."

"Yes."

"But you cannot travel to the *salasch* often now that you must carry on with your father's business."

Georg nodded.

Mammi stepped over to the table and removed the tea towels that covered the plates of cookies. "My women's shoes are taking up more and more of my time, and I have less to show Luki: he will never embroider. With Lukas coming home in two months, our son can wait to learn his father's trade. If you need some time away from your family, you are welcome here, both you and Eva, so long as you, Georg, take care of Luki. With Stefan working at the church now, he has less time for Luki, and my son needs another man in his life to teach and guide him." She folded the last tea towel. "So help me God, that is you."

Luki ran at Georg and hugged him tight.

Mammi lifted a plate in each hand. "But do *not* teach him how to ride on a horse. I do not need to hear more rumours about my family at church. Herr Meier has enough fodder with the help you give us in my husband's absence."

Rosina stamped her foot. "That's not fair! He also likes us!"

Georg smiled. "Yes, I do."

"Then you have to teach us things, too!"

Elisabeth knew she had to step in before Mammi's stern manner returned and the younger sisters got out of hand. "He will be very busy with blacksmithing. You can bake for him and Eva. Remember?"

A hint of mischief shone in Georg's eyes. "That would

be nice, but I wonder... If I can't teach your brother to ride in a saddle, perhaps I can teach your sisters?"

Elisabeth's hand flew to her mouth to cover her grin. Although it was more unusual than unacceptable for a man to ride on a horse, it was *un*acceptable and indeed *highly* inappropriate for a girl or a woman to ride a horse.

Mammi gasped and almost dropped the plates of cookies, "You will not—!"

But before she could finish her sentence, everyone broke into laughter. Elisabeth dropped her hand from her face as she joined in. Deep down, though, she was more stunned than happy: she couldn't remember Georg ever telling a joke. Had her siblings helped with this small change? Only time would tell.

All the people in the room were laughing so hard that even Mammi let a smile creep onto her face.

Elisabeth's siblings hugged Georg again, and Eva's eyes welled up.

"There is no need to worry, Lissa-Néni. I promise to look after your family as long as I live."

Elisabeth had no doubt he would keep his word.

CHAPTER TWENTY-ONE

"How did you like Claire's tea?" Juliana asked her cousin.

Sophie shrugged. "It wasn't bad. You?"

"Same. A little bitter, but the flower part was interesting. I guess you have to get used to it. My mom and your mom said they really liked it. It smelled nice."

"Like a garden."

Dad chimed in. "I surprisingly loved the one she recommended for me. It did help me focus on my courses this week."

All three fell silent and stared at the ground, where a stone grave marker lay in the grass. Dad had found an online listing of old gravestones in Kitchener from the local genealogy group. Juliana invited Sophie along, and they now stood in Woodland Cemetery, where Oma's grave was, too, along with the graves of many other Germans. Quite a few people seemed to be paying their respects. Given that it was Father's Day, that made sense.

Dad burped. "Looks like I'm still digesting that phenomenal breakfast your mother and aunt cooked."

Juliana held a bouquet so all she could do was wrinkle her nose. "TMI, Dad!"

Sophie covered her ears. "Yup, your dad wins for the weirdest in the clan."

Dad chuckled at the girls' reactions. "This is why I'm a dad. Well, and an uncle. Your dad's too normal, Sophie. I think I need to rub off on him a bit more."

But breakfast had been amazing. Aunt Anne had invited everyone to her house and she and Mom had cooked the most elaborate Father's Day breakfast Juliana had ever eaten: homemade bread and cinnamon buns; the requisite eggs, bacon, and hash browns; and a fruit flan topped with fresh strawberries and whipped cream, served with both kinds of tea the girls had brought home from Claire's Tea Shop. Opa didn't drink Georg's tea, but he didn't complain about its scent either. He tried Dad's green tea instead and seemed to enjoy it.

Because today was her year-end show, Juliana had to watch how much she ate: trying to dance after eating that much food felt like you were somersaulting with rocks in your stomach. But she ate a little of everything. Well, except for the flan. She ate a lot of that. But what was a fruit flan other than thick bread with some sugar on top and a fruit salad with some dairy, right?

Dad rubbed his belly. "I hear green tea helps your body burn fat more efficiently."

Sophie snorted and Juliana shook her head.

"I wonder if Georg had 'dad humour,'" Sophie said.

Juliana knelt down and ran her fingers over the stone grave marker, warmed by the sun. "It says 'George Shoemaker, March 30, 1890 to February 2, 1976.'" She did a little math in her head. "So he was twenty-nine at the start of the sketchbook Elisabeth's dad gave to her."

Sophie kneeled down beside Juliana and also touched the carved marker. She surveyed the cemetery. "But why does he only have this flat stone instead of something that stands up, Uncle Paul?"

Dad shrugged. "Gravestones are expensive. Something like this costs a lot less. Maybe he didn't have a lot of money."

Juliana held the bouquet of carnations and baby's breath out to Sophie. They had picked it up at Mom's grocery store on the way here. It wasn't anything fancy, but both girls could afford it: they had insisted on buying it with their own allowance. As stressful as Juliana's move had been, and as wild as Sophie's family could sometimes be, they both realized that without Georg, they wouldn't be here in Kitchener right now.

Sophie grasped the stems of the flowers below Juliana's

hand, and the girls slowly placed the bouquet on Georg's grave. They then stood up.

"He was a dad, but in a different way," Sophie said. "It's really sad what happened to his family."

"It doesn't sound like he was a very happy person. With all that pain, is it possible to be happy?" Juliana looked to Dad for a response, hoping he didn't mind being asked.

He wrapped his arm around Juliana. "The hard part about living with such an extreme case of mental illness is that people remember you for your sadness, not the moments of happiness that creep through. I don't know if he told dad jokes to anyone, but I'm sure he smiled from time to time, maybe even cracked a joke in some quiet way. My dad did."

The girls wiped their eyes. Juliana had never met this man, but just learning about him and the pain he went through moved her more than she had expected. In a sense, she owed him her life.

Dad added, "It's what war does to a family. To millions of families, actually. All those refugees from Syria we accepted a few years ago? I'm certain they're going through the same thing. And what about those coming from Africa? Other parts of the Middle East? Even parts of Asia?"

"It's like this World War taught us nothing," Sophie said. "Sixteen million dead and we're still fighting."

Dad's face became earnest. He placed his hands on Sophie's shoulder and looked her square in the eyes. "Don't ever say that, Sophie. Not everyone took their lessons from the World Wars: many people in the world believe that things will end differently for them if they go to war for their cause. But that doesn't mean that people like you and me and Juliana can't show compassion to others because we know these stories. We may not be able to change what's happening across the world, but we can change what's happening right here. Even just smiling at people you pass by on the street is an act of compassion."

Sophie nodded in acknowledgement, and Dad lowered his hands.

"Georg's idea of family was bigger than ours," he said. "I'm certain that in his mind, you both were his family, even though he didn't know you would ever exist."

Everyone remained silent for a few minutes as they stared at Georg's gravestone. The sun shone high in the sky, and birds flew from tree to tree, singing their songs. It seemed almost too happy for such a sad place. But maybe, just as people didn't always remember someone's happy side, it was harder to remember happy memories in a cemetery. Juliana was sad that she never got to meet Georg, but the more she thought about it, without the sacrifices he'd made, she realized she wouldn't have all the happy memories she carried with her, from sleepovers with Rachel to winning at dance competitions to becoming closer to her father over these past couple of weeks.

"Anything you'd like to say to him before we leave?"

Dad asked them. "We need to get Juliana to the theatre for her show in about an hour."

Juliana raised an eyebrow. "In *about* an hour? That doesn't sound very efficient." She placed a hand on Dad's forehead. "Are you feeling okay?"

Sophie laughed.

Dad chuckled. "Ha ha, very funny. I'm fine. I'm just trying to take to heart a few of your suggestions. So, yes. In *about* an hour."

Juliana faced Georg's gravestone again and stuck her hands in her skirt pockets. "I think I'd like to say something, though it feels weird."

"Maybe he's listening somehow," Sophie said, "and now he'll know that he did the best he could and that we're not angry with him."

Juliana nodded. "All right. So, Cousin Georg—or do you like being called George?" She looked at her father. "What do I call him?"

Dad squeezed her arm. "Whatever is comfortable for you, sweetheart."

Juliana took a deep breath as she thought about his name and spoke when she had an answer. "Cousin Georg—that's what your family called you—thank you for coming here."

Sophie nodded. "Yeah. Thanks. Because of you, I have five really weird siblings—but we care about each other. And I've got this awesome cousin." She hugged Juliana.

"And I know Opa didn't always like you, but I think he's changed his mind."

"I think so, too."

"Yeah."

"Yeah. So...we're really sorry about how hard life was for you. If you were alive today, we'd make sure you got the help you needed. Right, Sophie?"

"Absolutely. You'd be like another uncle to us."

"And...Happy Father's Day."

"Yeah. Happy Father's Day."

Juliana did her best to remember where Georg was buried so she could come back at Christmas. All three walked over the grass past a few other gravestones toward the car.

"I still don't understand why Opa hated him so much," Sophie said. "We have so much to thank him for."

"It's more about pride," Dad said. "Your grandfather puts family first and believed that Georg had failed at that. Then people start to remember only the stories about someone that fit their belief. I'm very certain that once your grandfather saw the truth, he really was sorry."

Before Juliana got in the car, she hugged Dad. "Happy Father's Day, Dad. I had no idea what you went through when you were younger. It's like these past weeks has been weeks of truth about dads."

Sophie got in on her side of the car and closed the door. "I learned something new this week, too," she said. "Mom is Dad's second wife. There was one before and she died from cancer not long after they were married. There weren't any kids. Mom and Dad never told anyone because they didn't really know when it would be a good time. Not even Rebecca knew. I guess Dad kept a picture of her in his wallet all these years, but Mom said that with all this honesty about the past, it was time to tell us, too. The beautiful thing is that there's now a large picture of her on the mantle in the family room."

"Your mom's okay with that?" Juliana asked.

"You should have heard the relief in her voice when she told us. Even Dad relaxed more afterwards. My parents have been married for almost twenty-five years. That's a long time to keep a big secret."

Dad pulled away from the side of the road and headed toward the cemetery exit. "Everyone carries some sadness around with them all the time. Some people, like your grandfather, protect it with anger. Others, like your dad, Sophie, hide the pain but take a peek now and then. Then there are those like Georg who run as far from it as they can." Dad shook his head in amazement. "That he survived for years after that war without...well, it's nothing short of a miracle."

Dad's voice wavered, and Juliana looked out the window. She didn't like it when her parents got too emotional in front of her.

Dad stopped at an intersection and turned to face the

girls. "I wonder if that's where both of you get some of your strength from to deal with the challenges life's thrown at you."

The cousins exchanged looks and then smiled at each other.

Gravestones of different shapes, sizes, and colours passed by as Dad followed the maze of roads.

"I guess that old factory meant a lot to us, too, didn't it?" Juliana asked.

Dad looked at her through the rear-view mirror. "It provided for your mom's family for much longer than anyone could have guessed."

"Do you think Opa will get cancer?" Sophie asked.

His eyes back on the road, Dad shrugged. "No one knows for sure, Sophie. But we can't spend our time worrying about the future. If you do, it takes away from enjoying today." Dad smiled. "That sort of rhymed."

He pulled on to the main street and headed home.

Juliana reached out for Sophie's hand and squeezed. "I'm so glad Georg came to Canada because otherwise you and I would have never met."

Sophie squeezed Juliana's hand back and beamed. "Heck, we would have never been born!"

Juliana's heart had never been so full. Her dancing this evening would be the best she'd ever done, because it would be inspired by the generations that came before her.

She'd dedicate her tap group to Georg, her ballet group

to her family, and her jazz group to the factory workers who had accepted her family as they built a life in Canada. It would be the first time that Juliana would truly dance for others, like Elisabeth had drawn for her father. But it wouldn't be the last time. She would make sure of that.

SETTING THE RECORD
STRAIGHT

Between Worlds tells a contemporary fictional story together with a story that is historical fiction. In both parts of the book, I've taken facts about life in the time period in which the story is set and included them in a fictional story. In writing novels, the story always comes first (because otherwise this would be a history textbook), so this section explains any important facts that may have been changed to fit the story and adds more background to the story. If you have any questions about what you've read in this, or in any of the other books in the series, ask away! My contact information is in the "Stay in Touch!" section.

BALLET COLOURS

Ballet originated in the Italian Renaissance, and its technique became formalized in the fifteenth and sixteenth centuries. It has since expanded to a worldwide following, with students of every skin colour and from every background imaginable dedicated to learning the art form. Sadly, though, ballet's insistence on dancers having white skin has remained persistent. This novel takes place in 2019, before the events of 2020 unfolded. So, if Juliana seemed a little naïve to you when she was talking to Jasmine about the colour of Jasmine's pointe shoes, that's why.

One area of ballet that continues to favour white skin is the traditional colours of tights and shoes. It's called "ballet pink." However, the colour has made many girls and women with dark skin feel uncomfortable for many, many reasons. You can look online to find personal essays and blog posts about it.

It wasn't until pointe shoe makers were publicly called out in 2020 that several pledged to make shoes available in a wider range of skin colours.

This systemic racism wasn't just in ballet pink, though. It was also in what I grew up knowing as "skin tone" tights. "Nude" and "tan" were also common names. Occasionally, they were more accurately called "beige." Even when I first wrote the colour of Jasmine's tights, my fingers began typing "tan," because that name was so engrained in me.

It was April 2021 as I drafted that scene and looked up what colour names were used for tights meant for darker skin tones. Sadly, the major dancewear company whose site I landed on (and one that was called out about its lack of diversity in pointe shoe colours) still called darker shades "tan" and "dark tan." In other words, they still used colours from a white dancer's perspective.

There are many online resources today that discuss ballet and the extremely outdated demand for white skin. Brown Girls Do Ballet is an organization whose mission is to help increase participation of underrepresented populations in ballet programs. That includes supporting girls (and women!) with dark skin with the resources needed to enjoy their chosen art form and excel in it to the best of their abilities while not being made to feel guilty that their skin is the wrong colour. You can learn more about the organization at their website: BrownGirlsDoBallet.com.

If you come across dancewear and shoes that still use names like "tan" and "dark tan," email the companies and let them know you'd like to see names that don't use shades of white skin as the name.

ALONE VS. LONELY

In Chapter 18, Elisabeth and Stefan try to express that Georg is lonely. However, there's a reason they don't say the word: it most likely didn't exist in their dialect.

I came across that fact in an interview with the Nobel Prize for Literature winner Hertha Müller, who is from a town not too far away from Semlak and speaks a dialect similar to what Elisabeth and her community would have spoken. Müller said that their dialect did not have a word for *lonely*.

German has a word for *lonely*: *einsam*. However, the dialects of German the Danube Swabians spoke may not have had that word. Although I'm not an expert in the dialect Elisabeth spoke, I don't recall my grandparents ever saying *einsam*. The German word for *alone* is *allein*, and in my grandparents' dialect that came out as *aalaanich*, but I have no recollection of something meaning *einsam*. I asked a few members of that cultural community, and they came to the same conclusion.

Although this should not be seen as a definitive conclusion about a group of dialects spoken by millions, I do find the observation interesting. Could it be that the communal life of the Danube Swabians meant they had no need for a word like *lonely*?

Do an online search for "words that don't exist in

English but should" and see what you find. I bet you'll come across some fun words!

STROKES

I lost my maternal grandfather (1922-1986) to a stroke. I wasn't yet nine years old, and I was sad for a long time.

A stroke happens when part of your brain doesn't get enough blood and therefore doesn't get enough oxygen and nutrients. There are many causes for this. You may know someone in your family who has had a stroke. Only recently has medicine been able to treat strokes and minimize the damage to the brain. But in Elisabeth's time, a stroke was essentially a death sentence.

If someone in your family has just had a stroke and you're scared about how that person will change, talk to a parent, guardian, teacher, or any other adult you trust about your feelings. We know so much more today than we did in Elisabeth's time. It's always best to ask and get the facts.

Learn the signs of a stroke from a trusted source, like a first-aid class or lifeguard training course, so you know what someone looks like when they're having a stroke and can call for help (911 in North America).

REMARRYING AFTER DEATH

In Elisabeth's culture, and I believe in many cultures around the world still today, a widow had to remarry to survive. The man of the house was the breadwinner—women like Mammi were few and far between—and without a husband, the woman had no way of earning a decent living. She could work as a day labourer for other farmers, but this made childcare very difficult.

My paternal grandfather (1929-2021) was raised by a single mom in a village called Gara, in Hungary. His father had passed away from refusing treatment for appendicitis because it was Easter weekend and he had a lot of shoe orders to fulfill. (The Schuhmacher family's profession was chosen to honour him.) By the time he allowed a doctor to examine him, it was too late, and his decision to wait until his work was done left my great-grandmother and grandfather without a man in the house when my grandfather was about four years old.

According to my grandfather's memoir, a man was interested in marrying my great-grandmother but she refused, because she feared her son would not be treated as well as the man's biological children. My grandfather grew up in poverty: his mother knew how to repair shoes but not make them, and when she helped with the harvest, a woman was paid less than a man. My grandfather once told me that smoked sausage was an annual treat for him: they couldn't afford it on a regular basis.

However, in Margarethe-Néni's case, as Elisabeth says, her children are grown and married, so it is now their job to support her. That responsibility usually rested on the shoulders of the oldest son, with whom the parents lived, though I'm certain exceptions were made.

THE RUBBER INDUSTRY IN WATERLOO REGION

The Regional Municipality of Waterloo is made up of three cities (Kitchener, Waterloo, and Cambridge) and four townships (Wilmot, Wellesley, Woolwich, and North Dumfries). This is where I live.

The area is known for its farmland and tech sector, but for about 150 years it was known for its manufacturing industry. My maternal family benefited from working at a factory that produced rubber and manufactured tires from it. My grandfather worked on the line and my grandmother in the canteen. It had always been my hope to interview people who used to work in these factories to weave their stories into this series. Although it's clear throughout the series that Opa, his friend Karl, and Uncle Peter all worked at a factory, I never went into deeper detail because I didn't have the information necessary. Thanks to a grant from the Region of Waterloo Arts Fund, my dream came true in this book.

I interviewed several men about their work in these factories and incorporated their stories into the novel. Their names are in the Acknowledgements section. If you visit my website, you'll find articles about the rubber industry in Waterloo Region, written from the interviews I conducted, plus other resources for further research.

STAY IN TOUCH!

If you enjoyed the book, sign up for my monthly newsletter! I write it myself, so it's my words to you. You'll get the following:

- Sneak peeks at upcoming books
- Updates about online and in-person appearances
- Book and writing recommendations
- Recipes I love
- Contests
- And more!

Visit BetweenWorldsYA.com to sign up!

Prefer social media? All my links are listed under my bio, at the end of the book.

COLLECT ALL THE BOOKS IN THE SERIES

Don't miss out on a single step in Juliana's and Elisabeth's journeys. You can order the books below from your favourite book store or online retailer.

AVAILABLE IN REGULAR PRINT, LARGE PRINT, AND EBOOK

1. The Move
2. The Distance
3. The First Step
4. What Friends Do
5. Hide and Seek
6. Missing Home
7. What Will Come
8. A Father's Journey
9. The last book! Coming in 2024.

Also check out my blog for more background information about the series. You'll read about some of the research that went into the book, discover more about the real Canadian neighbourhoods used in the book, and learn about writing. Visit www. BetweenWorldsYA.com.

ACKNOWLEDGEMENTS

I never work alone on a book, but more people helped me with this book than with any previous book in the series. Without their contributions, guidance, and feedback, this story would not have made it into your hands.

Every novel in *Between Worlds* incorporates oral history usually from my family's stories, and sometimes from stories of friends and acquaintances who share my cultural background. However, thanks to a grant from the Region of Waterloo Arts Fund, I could expand the scope of oral history in the novel to include stories of former rubber workers from Waterloo Region. So thank you to Wayne, Dan, Jim, Mark, Don, Glenn, Eric, Don, and Brian for sharing your stories with me. Visit loriwolfheffner.com for a few articles based directly on our conversations.

Thank you to Aniyah Stuart-Veira for her feedback on the scene in Chapter 3 where Juliana learns how Jasmine prepares her pointe shoes so they match her brown skin.

You'll see this group mentioned in every book: the

Donauschwaben Villages Helping Hands, a non-profit organization whose online resources, members, and volunteers help me find the information I need to portray Elisabeth and her family as accurately as possible for you.

I also frequently use the book *Semlak: Ein Heimatbuch*, edited by Georg Schmidt and published by the Heimatortsgemeinschaft Semlak in 2016, to recreate Semlak in 1920 to the best of my abilities.

Over the past three years, I've enlisted the help of Gabriela Rat and Crenguta Nicolae in Romania and Daniel Kalman and Levente Csibi in Hungary to help with more in-depth research and translation. Their research has helped me fill in some gaps caused by my lack of knowledge of Romanian and Hungarian.

I certainly can't write a book about a teenage dancer without having danced myself. Thank you, Deardra King-Leslie, and my many other dance teachers, for guiding me through all those years of dance.

Thank you to my book team: Michelle Fairbanks (book cover designer), Heather Wright (consulting editor and mentor), ali macgee (mentor), Susan Fish (editor), and Jennifer Dinsmore (proofreader). Any remaining errors are mine.

And, of course, thank you to my family: Mom, Dad, and Kristin, for believing in me and supporting me all these years. Thank you to Corey, for your love. You probably didn't know you'd married a reclusive writer! And thank you to Khristopher and Jonnathan for all your patience as this book, and all the others, get written in Mommy's office.

Photo by Erin Watt Photography

Lori Wolf-Heffner is a former competitive dancer, dance teacher, and theatre manager. She was a member of the first Canadian National Tap Team, back in 1996, under the leadership of Bonnie Dyer, with choreographer Mathew Clark. She's written for *Dance Canada Quarterly*, *just dance!* magazine, and *The Dance Current* (all under Lori Straus).

Fluent in German, Lori lived in Germany for three years, never once realizing just how close she was to some of the villages her ancestors left to migrate to Eastern Europe in the 1700s.

Lori lives in Waterloo, Ontario, Canada, with her husband and two sons. She is a member of The Writers' Union of Canada and the Alliance of Independent Authors.

facebook.com/loriwolfheffner
x.com/LoriWolfHeffner
instagram.com/loriwolfheffner
goodreads.com/lori_wolf-heffner
bookbub.com/author/lori-wolf-heffner
pinterest.com/loriwolfheffner
amazon.com/author/loriwolfheffner

9 781989 465240